I went down to the stream, dropped my clothes on a bush, set my gunbelt down on a rock, and dove in.

I was splashing around for a couple of minutes, washing the trail grit from my skin and thinking about how only a moment ago there were three lovely, naked women bathing where I was now. Suddenly I felt someone come up behind me. I felt arms snake around my waist and smelled the fine scent of a woman.

"Sara?" I asked.

"You're not surprised?" she said, biting my ear from behind.

"I am, but I'm not. What would we tell your mother if she came back?"

"Why tell her anything?" the girl whispered seductively. "Why talk at all?"

DON'T MISS THESE ALL-ACTION WESTERN SERIES FROM THE BERKLEY PUBLISHING GROUP

THE GUNSMITH by J. R. Roberts

Clint Adams was a legend among lawmen, outlaws, and ladies. They called him . . . the Gunsmith.

LONGARM by Tabor Evans

The popular long-running series about U.S. Deputy Marshal Long—his life, his loves, his fight for justice.

LONE STAR by Wesley Ellis

The blazing adventures of Jessica Starbuck and the martial arts master, Ki. Over eight million copies in print.

SLOCUM by Jake Logan

Today's longest-running action western. John Slocum rides a deadly trail of hot blood and cold steel.

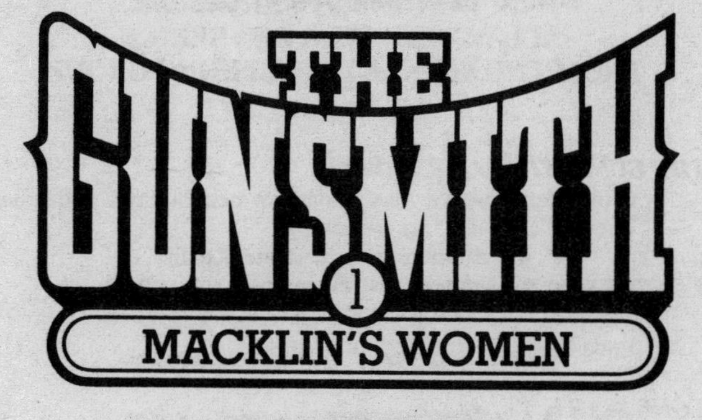

J.R. ROBERTS

JOVE BOOKS, NEW YORK

To Bob Randisi, without whom this book would not have been possible.

All characters in this book are fictitious.
Any resemblance to actual persons, living or dead,
is purely coincidental.

THE GUNSMITH #1: MACKLIN'S WOMEN

A Jove Book / published by arrangement with
the author

PRINTING HISTORY
Ace edition / January 1982
Jove edition / November 1988

ISBN: 0-515-10145-1

Jove Books are published by The Berkley Publishing Group,
200 Madison Avenue, New York, New York 10016.
The name "JOVE" and the "J" logo
are trademarks belonging to Jove Publications, Inc.

PRINTED IN THE UNITED STATES OF AMERICA

10 9 8 7 6 5 4 3 2

1

I wasn't quite sure where I was.

The reason for that was because I was looking at two signposts. The first sign read:

BAXTERVILLE, MO.
Population 500

The second, older sign read:

I was about to enter Baxterville, Missouri, which had until recently been called Macklinville—a name which rang a bell. I sat a moment, searching through my memory, but when nothing came to mind, I put it aside.

With a flick of my wrists I set my team in motion and me and my rig were on our way into Baxterville, Mo., population 500.

I wondered idly what had happened to the other ten.

When I entered the town proper I asked the first man I saw where the livery stable was. I was anxious to put up my team and rig and make sure that Duke, my big, half-Arabian stallion—who was tied to the rear of the wagon—was cared for. After that I wanted a couple of beers, a bath, a few more beers with some food, and then some female companionship.

As I approached the livery, halfway across the town, a blonde girl was closing the doors, apparently shutting down for lunch.

"Excuse me," I called out to her.

"Yeah?" she answered, turning and, hands on formidable hips, squinting into the noonday sun as she attempted to make out my face.

She appeared to be barely eighteen, but she had the full breasts and proud bearing of a grown woman. Her wheat-colored hair was long and fine, and the same color eyelashes made her appear to have none at all. A cluster of freckles played across the bridge of her nose, which wrinkled up as she continued peering at my face. She had a wide mouth. All that marred her wholesome good looks was the absence of one of her front teeth. It did little, however, to damage her overall appeal.

I stepped down from the wagon, so as to save her further difficulty with the sun. Once I was on the ground she was able to take a good, frank look at me. What she saw was a tall, lean man covered with trail dust and a week's worth of stubble. Cleaned up, I might have been called pleasant-looking but at the moment I looked like hell.

"Kin I help ya?" she asked.

"Well, I'd like to put up my rig and have my animals cared for, but I see that you're closing up. For lunch?"

"S'right. Paw's laid up with a broke leg, so I got to close up to eat, or I don't eat," she explained.

"I see. Well," I began, scratching my head like I was pondering a major problem, "I can't very well leave my horses and rig standing out here, can I?"

"Not if'n you want them to be here when you get back."

"Say," I said, hoping I looked like I had just gotten the best idea since the wheel, "I'll tell you what . . . uh, what's your name?"

"Lizzie."

"I'll tell you what, Lizzie. If you'll put up my rig and care for my horses, I'll buy you the biggest lunch you ever had. How's that sound?"

Without hesitation she said, "That sounds right nice, Mister."

"Clint."

"Clint, are you sure you kin afford it?" she asked, eyeing me doubtfully. "I'm a right big eater when I'm hungry, and right now I'm powerful hungry," she warned.

"With a figure like yours? I would have thought that you hardly ate a thing all day."

"That's nice of you, Clint, but truth be told, I'm kind of a big girl and it takes a lot of food to keep me going. Paw says he's seen me eat more than some of the horses we put up here."

Talking about her own figure caused her to suck in her tummy some, which caused her impressive breasts to stand out all the more. I had to agree with Lizzie. She certainly was a big girl, and that was just the way I liked them.

"I can afford it," I assured her. "What do you say?"

"I'll take care of your animals and then meet you at Hobson's saloon, just down the block. After that we kin go over to the cafe for that big lunch."

"Let me drive the rig inside," I offered.

She opened the doors wide and I guided the team inside, then hopped down and told her, "Take special care of the Duke, here."

She came over next to me and said, "He shore is a beautiful animal. Got a plain name for such a fancy lookin' horse," she added.

"Duke likes it," I assured her. I'd had Duke for four years, since he was a yearling, and by now we were pretty much able to read each other's minds. "He likes it just fine, don't you boy?"

He nuzzled my hand, then showed good taste by nuzzling Lizzie's as she patted his massive neck.

I cupped Lizzie's chin and said, "Don't be long. I'm almost as hungry as you are."

"I'll be right along," she promised.

It looked like I had found everything I wanted all in one place.

Outside the livery I noticed that there had also been a sign change there, recently. The sign that was up now was clean and new and declared that I had just left the Baxterville Livery. On the way to the saloon I passed the general store, where two men were taking down a sign that said MACKLIN'S GENERAL STORE and preparing to put one up that said SMITH'S GENERAL STORE.

When I reached the saloon I saw a large sign lying in the street, where it had been trampled a few dozen times. It was upside down, but I was able to make out the words MACKLIN'S SALOON. Above the doorway was a new sign which said HOBSON'S SALOON.

Somebody named Macklin must have had quite a run of bad luck.

I walked into the saloon, which wasn't exactly overcrowded at that time of day. There were four cowpokes playing poker at one table, and a lone drunk at another, sucking on a bottle. I walked up to the bar and ordered a beer.

"Just ride in?" the bartender asked.

I told him I had and accepted the beer from his big hand.

He was not a tall man, but he had large shoulders and thick, powerful hands. Handy in a bar fight, I figured.

I drank half of the beer and set it on the bar, saying, "Ah, that cuts through the dust nicely."

"Finish it up," he told me, "And have another on the house."

"That's right nice of you," I told him, and downed the remainder of the beer.

He drew me another. "We're kind of celebrating this week."

"New owner?" I asked.

"Kind of. I guess you noticed a few changes going on around town?"

"Oh, you mean the sign changes. I noticed that even before I got into town."

"Well, we're celebratin' gettin' our town back from Con Macklin," the bartender told me proudly.

"Con Macklin," I repeated, and then the name struck that cord inside my head. "Con Macklin!" I said again, this time because it meant something. The memory went back about ten years, but it was coming into sharp focus. I'd never met Macklin, but I had seen my share of Wanted posters with his name on them while I was a lawman in Kansas, Wyoming and Texas, among other places. He was a gunman, but one of the smarter ones. He stayed alive and out of jail long enough to disappear from sight, about two years ago. Now I knew where he went.

Baxterville, Mo., to turn it into Macklinville, Mo.

From the looks of things, it had taken the people of the town two years to turn it back into Baxterville.

"You've heard of him, huh?" the bartender asked.

"I've heard the name," I admitted. "This was his town, eh?"

" 'Was' is the right word, Mister. We run him out."

"He must have had some men with him. What happened to them?"

"Gone. Guess you noticed the drop in our population. On the sign."

"Decreased by ten. Macklin and his men?"

"Macklin and his men made up seven. There's three more in town, but they'll be leavin' before the day is out."

He seemed pretty definite about that.

"What made Macklin and his boys pull out?" I asked.

"New sheriff," he said, proudly, which made me wonder if the new sheriff might not be his son. "He ran Macklin out of town, killed him, buried him, and then came back and told Macklin's boys. Damned if they didn't pull right out the next day."

"With nobody to pay them off, why should they stay?" I remarked.

"That's it, Mister."

Sheriff must be quite a guy.

"Who's the new sheriff?"

"Dade Whitman."

I put my beer down on the bar so I wouldn't spill any of it.

"Dade Whitman is your new sheriff?" I asked slowly, hoping I had heard wrong.

"You a friend of his?" he asked me.

I decided to be real careful about my answer, because Whitman had obviously become a big man in this town awful fast.

"I wouldn't exactly say that Dade and I were old friends, but we have worked together once or twice. Where exactly is Macklin buried?" I asked.

"In the hills somewhere," he answered, as if the exact location was of no concern to him at all. "Sheriff Whitman didn't even mark his grave, 'cause who'd wanna visit it? Just what he deserved, too, that's what I say."

"You're probably right."

At that point the swinging saloon doors opened to admit three women. I saw them through the mirror behind the bar, and then turned to take a better look.

One was older than the other two, maybe in her early to middle thirties. She was a tall redhead with her hair piled high atop her head, like a crown. She wore a blue dress and filled it out proudly with well-rounded breasts. Her face wasn't the most beautiful I'd ever seen, but it certainly ranked among the top ten. In addition to all that, a sensuous aura surrounded her that made a man lick his lips.

The other girls were not yet twenty. One was blonde, with a figure similar to the older woman's. The third was dark-haired, the youngest of the three, with a very pretty face and a slim figure. The two younger girls were wearing pants and boots and men's shirts.

The older woman was the one who spoke.

"I'm lookin' for a man to act as a guide to Mexico," she announced. "I'll pay good wages, half now and the other have when we get there."

The way the three of them looked, I expected every man in the place to volunteer, but no one moved and one man from the poker table said, "Get the hell out, bitch."

Another man added, "Take your whores with you."

The red-headed woman threw them a hard glance and I stood up straighter, sensing trouble.

"Look," she tried again, "we want to get out of this town but we can't make the trip alone. I said I'd pay good wages—"

One of the men stood up from the poker table. He was big, over six feet, with "hardcase" written all over him. He approached the three women and drawled, "Well now seems to me if you're willin' to pay good wages, you might be willin' to throw in a little somethin' extra. Like mebbe this here little blonde lady," he added, grabbing the blonde around the waist.

"Let go!" she shouted, beating him on the chest with ineffective punches.

"C'mon, girlie, I jest wanna check you out and see if you're for real." He cupped one of her firm breasts in his big hand.

"Let her go," the older women demanded. She punctuated the demand by ramming a spiked heel into the man's instep. He howled and turned the blonde loose, then threw a backhand at the redhead, catching her high on her cheek. It was only because the dark-haired girl steadied her that she didn't fall.

"Get out, you whore, and take your little bitches with you before I kill you!" the man spat at her.

I'd had about enough and started to move forward when the bartender grabbed my arm.

"Mister, those are Con Macklin's women, and if you stand up for them, you're gonna be a mighty unpopular fella in this town. Take my advice and just let it ride, huh?"

I stayed undecided long enough for the situation to resolve itself. The woman turned and walked out of the saloon rubbing her cheek, and the two young girls followed. I caught the eye of the blonde just before she left, and our gazes held a few seconds before she tilted her chin and marched out.

"Have another beer, Mister," the bartender told me.

I watched the big man limp back to his seat, where his friends laughed and patted him on the back. Then I turned and accepted the beer.

"Can't stand to see women mistreated, especially pretty ones," I told him.

"They're pretty, all right, no denyin' that, but they were Macklin's women, Mister. Ain't nobody gonna take her up on her offer not even if it meant findin' Macklin's treasure."

"His treasure?"

"Sure. Everybody always wondered what Macklin did with his money. They figured he socked it away somewhere, and people started callin' it Macklin's buried treasure. Now that he's dead, that redhead might be the only one who knows where it's hid." He leaned on the bar and lowered his voice. "Now ain't nobody gonna guide her on the road to Mexico, but there might be some who'd be waitin' for her, if you get my meanin'."

I did, and told him so without any satisfaction.

"Them gals won't last two hours once they leave town," the bartender added, "and all I got to say is good riddance. Once they're gone this town will be shuck of any reminder that Con Macklin was ever in this town."

I threw some money on the bar—enough for the beers and a little extra—and said, "Thanks for the drinks, pal, and the advice. Where can I get a bath and a shave?"

"Go out, make a left. When you get to the hardware store, make another left, you'll see it. Big sign outside says 'baths for ten cents.' When Macklin was here, they was two bits and he was takin' a cut, but that's all changed now."

"Thanks to Dade Whitman," I added.

"That's right."

Sure it is, I thought. Until Dade Whitman decided to assert himself a little.

"I'm meeting a lady here by the name of Lizzie," I told him. "Would you tell her where I went?"

"Sure." He made eyes at me and said, "That Lizzie, if she cottons to you enough to meet with you as soon as you hit town, you're in for some night, yes, sir."

"Yeah, thanks."

When I left the saloon the men at the poker table were

still ribbing their friend about his sore foot. I took another look at him, although there was no danger that I'd ever forget what he looked like. Any man who would treat a woman the way he did left an impression on my mind—the kind that never faded.

2

After a bath and shave I was ready for that big lunch I had promised Lizzie. Approaching the saloon, I grew aware of some commotion inside. It sounded like one or more of the Macklin women had returned, and was being given a hard time.

When I entered I saw that I was half right. It wasn't a Macklin who was being given a hard time, but it was a woman. It was Lizzie, and she was being manhandled by the same guy who had struck the redheaded Macklin woman.

"C'mon, Lizzie, you and me, we could have some fun together," he was telling her. He was holding her by the arm, and from the way she was wincing I could tell it hurt.

"Let her go," I said aloud.

The big man switched his gaze from Lizzie to me and said, "What did you say?"

The big man's friends also looked from Lizzie to me, with open curiosity. The bartender put a hand over his eyes and shook his head, but I could only see one hand. His other was beneath the bar.

"You heard me, friend," I told the big man. "You may be stupid, but I don't think you're deaf," I told him.

One of the other men gave a crooked laugh and asked me, "Do you know who you're talkin' to, pard?"

"No, as a matter of fact I don't. All I see is a big man with a big mouth who likes to pick on women." I directed myself at the man we were talking about and said, "Now let go of her arm. The lady and I have a date for lunch."

"Lady?" he laughed. "Did you say lady? Pal, this ain't no lady, and I just broke your date, so why don't you—"

"Maybe I was wrong, friend," I told him. "Maybe you are deaf as well as stupid. Let the girl go. Watch my lips move. Let . . . her . . . go!"

The man's face hardened and he released Lizzie's arm and shoved her aside. He turned his body so that he was facing me and let his right hand hang by his gun.

"Mister, you're lookin' for a fast trip to your grave, and I'm the man who can give it to you."

His friends moved out of the line of fire in a hurry, so I didn't think I was going to have to deal with them.

"Listen, friend," I said, "I don't like to kill a man without knowing his name. I consider it bad luck, you know? So, what's your name?"

I sensed some movement behind him, and started to realize that maybe I was wrong about his friends. By now the room was so quiet that we all heard the sound of the hammer of a revolver as it was being cocked. If I wasn't mistaken, it had come from beneath the bar, where the bartender's right hand was.

"You and me, friend," I told the big man, figuring that the bartender had the rest of them covered.

"What's your name?" I asked him again.

"Shagan."

"Okay, Shagan. Apologize to the lady and nobody has to get hurt. It's as simple as that."

The tension in the air was like something solid. I kept

my eyes on Shagan's, waiting for him to make a move. His eyes would tell me what that move would be.

When one of his hands finally moved, it went to the buckle of his gunbelt, undid it and let it drop to the floor.

"I don't need my gun to take care of you," he said.

There wasn't much difference in our height, but he outweighed me by a good thirty pounds or so. He had more confidence in his ability to beat me to a pulp than he did in his ability to beat me to the draw.

I let my gunbelt drop to the floor and waited for him to move. He was predictable. Most men that size will try and use their weight against you. In his case, he ran towards me, meaning to throw himself on me and topple me to the floor.

I decided not to take any chances with him. I picked up a chair and hit him over the head with it. He fell to the floor, bleeding from a gash on his forehead, just barely conscious.

"You better help him up and take him out," I told his friends, bending to retrieve my gunbelt and buckle it on.

I walked over to Lizzie and asked, "Are you all right?"

From behind me I could hear them dragging him to his feet and helping him outside.

"I'm fine," she told me. "Thanks."

"I'm hungry," I told her. "I didn't want anything to delay that lunch we had planned."

I turned to the bartender and said, "What's your name?"

"Sam Hobson."

"Mr. Hobson, I want to thank you for backing me up."

"My pleasure," he told me, "but it would have been kind of hard to do if they had called my bluff."

"How's that?"

He reached under the bar and put an old Navy Colt on top of it.

"This piece is busted; it can't fire. I use it as a club. About the only other thing I can do with it is cock the hammer."

"Well, Sam," I told him, "that was enough, wasn't it?"

3

When Lizzie and I left the saloon to go to lunch, I took Sam Hobson's Navy Colt with me, promising to repair it.

Over lunch Lizzie warned me. "You made a bad enemy in Shagan, Clint."

"That's my lookout," I told her. "Just enjoy your lunch and don't worry about it."

I was doing Lizzie a disservice. I was having lunch with her, but I was thinking about the blonde that had been in the saloon, about the look she had given me before marching out.

"Clint?"

"Hm, yeah?" I answered, hoping she hadn't noticed my mind wandering.

"You got an awful lot of guns in that wagon of yours."

"You looked in my wagon?"

She shrugged, saying, "I was curious. You ain't mad, are you?"

"No, Lizzie, I'm not mad. I have all those guns because that's my business. I repair them, and sometimes I sell them."

"So that's why you tole Sam you'd fix his, huh?"

"That's right."

Watching her eat, I couldn't help but agree with her father. She did eat more than a lot of horses I'd seen. Had she eaten less, her figure might have rivaled that of the other blonde, but as it was she ran a bit on the plump side, while the other girl's figure was much firmer.

Not that I was complaining, mind you, just comparing.

Lizzie's face wasn't exactly pretty, but it was pleasant, in a clean, well-scrubbed way, despite the missing tooth. Her hair smelled faintly of the livery.

"You're very pretty, Lizzie," I told her.

"Thanks. You're not so bad yourself."

"May I call on you before I leave town?"

"You leavin' soon?" she asked, sounding disappointed. I hoped it wasn't only the prospect of losing further free lunches that made her sound that way.

"Within a day or so, I imagine," I told her.

She put her fork down, having finished her lunch, and told me, "Then I guess we ain't got any time to waste, do we?"

"I guess not," I agreed, surprised by her boldness.

"We can't go to my house tonight, seein' as how Paw's laid up and all. Why don't you come to the livery after dark?" she suggested.

"That sounds fine, Lizzie," I agreed, glad that we had avoided the usual fencing.

"I got to get back to work, Clint, but I'll see you tonight. Thanks a lot for lunch."

"You're welcome, Lizzie," I told her, and watched her trot from the cafe. She was like a big, healthy filly, which was one of the prettiest sights in this world.

Paying for lunch I realized how low my finances were getting. I was going to have to do something about that.

That was when I started thinking seriously about the Macklin woman's offer.

I knew the way to Mexico, and I knew there was some

rough terrain in the Southwest. If I didn't guide them, no one in this town would, and they'd end up dead, one way or another. Given the way the three of them looked, that would be a damn shame. Also, while I was keeping those three extremely good-looking women alive, I could be earning good wages as well.

And if I just so happened to stumble on Macklin's treasure as well, that would be okay, too.

Leaving the cafe, well-fed and satisfied with my plans, I wondered how I could locate the three of them, now. The problem solved itself when the smaller, dark-haired girl came out of the General Store across the street. She was carrying a couple of packages, and was not having an easy time of it.

I crossed the street and called out, "Excuse me."

When she turned her head the first thing I noticed were her eyes, which I had not seen that well in the saloon. They were large, like a doe's, and beautiful. They seemed to take up her whole face, distracting your attention from her small nose and lovely, rosebud mouth.

"Me?" she asked, obviously surprised that anyone in town would speak to her.

"Yes, you. May I help you with your packages?"

"Uh, I'm not goin' all that far, Mister—"

"That's all right," I assured, taking the packages from her arms.

"I'll walk along with you," I told her.

"Well, thank you," she stammered.

As we walked I said, "You were in the saloon earlier today, looking for a guide to Mexico, weren't you?"

"That's right."

"Well can we talk about that?"

"Uh, I guess you'd have to talk to my Maw about that."

"Is that where we're going now?" I asked.

"Yes." She indicated the packages I was now carrying and said, "We're packin' for the trip, and we needed some more supplies."

"Good, then I'll talk to your mother as soon as we get to where we're going."

Which turned out to be the hotel—which had a brand new sign over the entrance, naturally.

"We have to be out by mornin'," she explained as we entered.

I ignored the dirty look I got from the desk clerk as I followed her up the steps, which gave me a chance to observe how well she filled out her jeans for such a small girl.

She used her key to enter the room, and we walked in on the other two women. The redheaded woman was wearing the same dress, and the blonde had on the same jeans—but nothing else.

"Oops," I said.

She was facing me, the blonde was, and I couldn't help but admire her jutting, firmly rounded breasts. She had large, pink nipples and in the deep valley between her breasts, a light sprinkling of freckles.

"Excuse me," I told her, bowing slightly, but not enough to lose sight of her charms.

"Cover yourself up, Sara," the older woman commanded.

"Yes, Ma," the blonde said, but her eyes met mine and held there while she reached for a shirt and put it on slowly. She was putting on a show for me so I felt obligated to watch as her breasts vanished from sight. Just before they did, however, I could have sworn that her nipples were hardening. The girl was not at all shy.

"Can I help you with somethin', Mister?" the older woman asked.

"He wants to—" the younger girl started, but the redhead cut her off.

"I asked him, Billie," she told her. To me she said, "Well?"

"I understand you're looking for a guide to Mexico," I told her.

"That's right."

"What are the wages?"

"Two hundred dollars, half now and the rest when we get there."

I shook my head, said, "Not enough," and started to leave.

"Wait a minute," she called out. "Don't you want to haggle some?"

I turned and told her, "I'm not much for haggling, ma'am. I figure that was your offer, and it's just not enough."

"All right, all right, hold on a second." She thought a moment, then said, "Four hundred, not one penny more."

"Done," I told her.

She looked at me shrewdly and remarked, "Not good at haggling, huh?"

"I didn't say I wasn't good at it," I told her, "just that I wasn't much for doing it."

She pressed her lips together tightly. "Can you use that?" indicating my gun.

"I should be able to, I made it."

"Is that a fact?" she said, peering closer at it.

"It is."

She regarded me silently for a few moments, while the two younger girls inspected me like I was a prize bull, or something. I took the opportunity to take a closer look at them, too.

The blonde was genuinely more beautiful than the other two, but there was that quality about the redhead that I'd noticed in the saloon, a quality that the blonde might very well acquire with age . . . and experience. The dark-haired girl was a delectable little thing and would probably stay that way all her life, while the charms of the other two would probably fade—or sag—with age.

"What's your name?" she asked.

"Clint Adams. What's yours?"

"My name is Kate Macklin. These are my daughters, Sara and Billie."

"Ladies," I said, tipping my hat. "If you'll forgive me for saying so, ma'am, and it's more truth than compliment, but you hardly look old enough to be the mother of these girls."

"Well, I am. Sara's eighteen, though she looks older. Billie's sixteen. I'm—well, I'm older than them, but probably not as old as you."

"I'd have to agree with that. When would you like to start, ma'am?"

"Sunup."

"You have a wagon?" I asked.

"We do, and supplies, which I thank you for carrying here. All you have to do is meet us out front and be ready to ride. You do have a horse, don't you?"

"Yes, ma'am, a very fine one."

"Very well. We'll see you in the morning, Mr. Adams."

"Good evening, ma'am, ladies," I said, and left the room, exchanging one more glance with Sara.

4

On the way out of the hotel I decided to stop at the desk and register.

"I'd like a room," I told the clerk.

"We're full up," he told me. He was the same man who'd given me the dirty look when I'd entered with Billie.

"I see some keys in the boxes, friend," I told him.

"They're reserved," he said tightly. Obviously, he objected to my having helped Billie with her packages.

"You're a liar, friend," I told him.

He seemed to draw back a little, but he wasn't afraid to speak up, even if he did only come up to my chin.

"I don't have to let you have a room if I don't want to, Mister. You're helpin' those Macklin women, which means you ain't welcome here. Now if you don't leave, I'll have to call for Sheriff Whitman," he told me, then repeated the name for effect, "Sheriff Dade Whitman."

It wasn't the threat of Dade Whitman that made me leave without another word, but the desire to avoid trouble. Besides, I was sure Lizzie wouldn't mind letting me spend the night in the livery stable.

I went back to the saloon and ordered a beer from Sam Hobson.

"I'll be leaving in the morning, Sam," I told him, "but

I'll drop off your Colt before I go."

"That's fine," he told me, setting the beer down in front of me.

I detected some coldness in his attitude. Word got around this town pretty fast. I mentioned that fact to him.

"I guess you ain't much for takin' advice, are you?" he asked.

"I need the money, Sam, it's as simple as that. Besides, I'll be leaving tomorrow and probably won't come back except to pick up my rig, so not being welcome in this town doesn't bother me all that much."

He thought about it a moment, then said, "I guess you're right, friend. Finish that up and I'll give you another."

"Thanks for understanding, Sam," I told him. I drank the beer and gave him the empty glass. "I've got some advice for you, now, Sam, which I'll give you as soon as you fill up that glass."

My back was to the room, but I was keeping watch through the mirror behind the bar. There was a poker game going on, but all of the players were different. The place had started to fill up as it closed in on evening, and the flashily dressed girls were making the rounds of the tables.

When Hobson came back with my beer I said, "Dade Whitman."

"What about him?" he asked, immediately on the defensive.

"Don't get defensive on me, Sam. I know Dade, and I just don't want you to expect too much of him. He's not the man you seem to think he is."

"You gotta be wrong, Mister. Dade Whitman saved this town and whatever he done before he came here ain't gonna change that. You start talkin' against the sheriff, you're gonna be even more unpopular than you are now," he warned.

Hobson went to the other end of the bar to serve someone else, as the place was filling up even more. I turned to survey the room, drink in hand, and as I did Sheriff Dade Whitman entered the room.

Our eyes met and held. I shifted my beer to my left hand, and waited for Dade to make his move.

"Hello, Adams," he greeted me. The room had gone totally quiet at his entrance, and now all eyes were trained on the two of us.

"Hello, Dade. You've come up in the world, I see. Made a big hero of yourself."

His eyes flicked around the room and then he said, "Not here. Finish your drink and let's go to my office."

"Sounds good," I told him. I finished my beer, slapped the mug down on the bar and said, "Let's go."

Whitman led the way down the street to his office, acknowledging the greetings of people as he went. I had no doubt but that he would ultimately turn the adulation of these people to his advantage. That was the kind of lawman Dade Whitman was, which was the reason we had never gotten along.

When we entered the Sheriff's Office—new sign, naturally, reading DADE WHITMAN, SHERIFF—Dade invited me to have a seat, and proceeded to seat himself imperiously behind his desk. He removed his hat and put his feet up. I grabbed a chair and pulled it in front of his desk.

"You're looking well," he told me. "What brings you to town? Still a lawman?"

"No, I gave that up, Dade. Retired."

"Gave up your star, huh? Never thought you'd do that."

"Yeah, well, neither did I," I admitted, but I refused to elaborate further for a man I didn't even like, let alone have respect for. "As for what I'm doing in town, I'm just passing through. I'll be leaving in the morning."

"Yeah, I heard about that," he told me. He dropped his feet off the desk, leaned forward and began playing with a pencil. "For someone who's been in town for just a little while you've become pretty unpopular, Clint. I hear you've agreed to escort the Macklin women to Mexico."

"And you're going to try and talk me out of it, is that it?" I asked him.

"No I'm not. I think it's a damned good idea. The sooner those women are out of my town, the better."

"I see."

"They're gonna need someone to protect them, and you've always been pretty handy with that gun of yours." He leaned over to peer at my holster and asked, "You still carry that one you made yourself?"

"I don't use it much anymore."

"Way I hear, you almost used it this morning."

"You mean Shagan."

"Shagan's a bad man with a gun, Clint. You made him back down, and then you crowned him with a chair." He frowned at me and said, "With a chair, Clint?"

I shrugged. "It was handy."

"Well, he's not likely to forget it. Just a friendly warning."

"Dade, I never remember us as being all that friendly. Why the change of heart?"

"Maybe I have had a change of heart." He sat back in his chair and said, "I'm sure you heard about what I did for these people. They look up to me, respect me."

"Because you killed Con Macklin and cleaned up their town."

"Because I gave them back their town."

The way I saw it, the town had simply changed hands, without the townspeople coming into it at all. It was Dade Whitman's now, whenever he chose to take it. Oh, he'd take his time, let the people become used to him, comfortable with him and then, slowly but surely, Dade Whitman would take over.

"You don't believe me, do you?" Whitman asked.

"To be perfectly honest, Dade, I don't, but I don't think that matters much. I'll be out of this town tomorrow and then you can do whatever you want with this town."

"You're right about that, Adams," he snarled, coming to his feet, "and you will be out of this town by tomorrow."

"Now that sounds like the old Dade Whitman," I told him, coming to my feet, too.

"I tried to be nice, Adams, but hear me good. I don't want you getting in my way."

"Don't worry, Dade. The last place on earth I want to be is in the same town as you."

"And stay away from Shagan. I don't want you killin' him before I get a chance to deputize him."

"You know, that figures," I told him. "If I had to pick one man in this town to be your deputy, it would be Shagan. Goodbye, Dade. I hope we don't meet again . . . ever!"

"If we do," he promised me, "it could be the last time."

Whitman was a big, rawboned man who wore two guns and knew how to use them. I had never actually gone up against him, but if that was what he wanted . . .

"That'll be your choice, Dade," I told him, and left.

5

I went to my rig at the livery to repair Sam Hobson's Navy Colt. When I had it fixed I brought it to him at the saloon and got another free drink for my trouble. I had a couple of more beers after that and when it started to get dark I said goodbye to Hobson and went to keep an important appointment.

When I entered the livery it was dark except for one lamp, and in the light from that lamp stood Lizzie. She had obviously been waiting for me and when she saw me she began to unbutton her dress.

"Lock the door," she told me. I did as she told me and then watched her undress. In the light from the lone lantern, she seemed to be standing in a moonbeam.

She had obviously prepared for this scene in advance, because she wore no undergarments at all. She slid the dress down over her shoulder, allowed it to drop to the floor, and then she was naked.

She had large, pendulous breasts, not as firm or as high as Sara Macklin's, but lovely nevertheless. It was a shame to think that in ten or fifteen years they would become misshapen from bearing their own weight. Right now they were smooth and white, the nipples penny brown and as hard as cherry pits. She had wide hips, heavy thighs and there was a slight swell to her belly.

She was a big girl, built for bed—or a pile of hay.

"Hurry, Clint," she urged me. "I been waitin'."

I didn't waste any time getting out of my clothes. When I approached her she took my hands and led me to a bed of hay she had prepared for us, and together we lay down.

Her tongue was alive in my mouth as we kissed. I used my own tongue to explore the gap where her front tooth was missing. My hands roamed from one breast to the other, teasing her nipples until they were like pebbles. She moaned into my mouth as her passion rose and reached down to grasp my erection. It wasn't overly large, I admit, but it was impressive enough to excite her even more. She broke the kiss and slid down until she was able to take me into her mouth. I held her head firmly with both hands as she went to work with her teeth, tongue and lips. I allowed her to bring me right to the brink before grasping her shoulders, turning her around and laying her back down on the hay bed. I kissed her mouth, then her neck, then continued to work my way down. I lingered at each breast for a short time, pulling gently on her nipples at first, then biting harder and taking as much of each breast into my mouth as I could. She was moaning and whispering, "God, yes, God, yes," as I worked my way down over the slight mound of her belly, over the blonde patch of hair until I reached the wet, warm essence of her. I worked away at her avidly as she writhed and bucked beneath me, crying out, "Oh, my God, yesss . . ." as she experienced her first orgasm of the night.

"Please," she implored, "now, do it now."

I raised myself above her, enjoying the sweet, clean scent of her body and plunged myself deep inside of her. I felt her close up around me like a wet fist, and her powerful legs wrapped around my waist, locking me in.

I drove myself in as far and as hard as I could and her

gasps were like little explosions in my ear. When the time came she lifted us both up off the ground, and we exploded together. As I emptied myself into her moist, hot cavity her nails raked my back and her legs tightened even more. When it was over we lay there locked together, totally drained.

"Lizzie, you're quite a girl," I told her, finally rolling off of her.

"You're not finished, are you?" she asked, breathlessly.

"Unless you can find some way to bring me back—"

"There's only one way," she told me, and then she was on me, her mouth and tongue alive on my flaccid penis. In seconds I began to swell up again and she took the length of me into her mouth hungrily.

She seemed bent on swallowing me whole and just when I thought she might succeed she let me slip from between her lips.

"From behind, darling," she whispered, turning herself around on her hands and knees and raising her butt high in the air, "Please, from behind . . . and deep!"

I rose up on my own knees, grasped her smooth, ample buttocks and rammed myself home. She bit her lip to keep from screaming as she bucked against me, in rhythm with my thrusts. Each time I thought I could go no deeper, I was surprised. This big, healthy girl seemed like a bottomless pit, and tireless as well.

"Wait!" she cried out suddenly. She moved forward so that my erection sprang loose, pulsing and prodding in the air. She rearranged us so that we both were face to crotch and then she took me in her mouth again and began to suck furiously. I buried my face in her wetness and began to return the favor with enthusiasm. That's the way we stayed until we each experienced another earth-moving explosion.

"You're incredible," I told her. "Insatiable."

"I don't know what that word means, Clint, but if it means that I love being with a man, then you're surely right." She snuggled up to me, brushing her breasts against my chest and asked, "More?"

I rolled my eyes up to heaven, but she was on me, and very soon, to my surprise, she had me ready again.

And that's how the night went.

6

"You comin' back this way, Clint?" Lizzie asked hopefully the following morning.

"I have to come back for my rig, Lizzie," I reminded her as I saddled up Duke. "You take good care of my things, okay?"

"Is that all you'll be comin' back for?" she asked sly-ly, her hand snaking down between my legs. I grabbed for her hand and held it. I was exhausted from the previous night, and I couldn't afford to have her get me started again.

"I swear, you are the hungriest little girl," I told her, then kissed her hard and let her go. "I'll be back soon enough, Lizzie, and then we'll see."

"I'll be a-waitin'," she promised.

I mounted Duke and rode out into the street. It was just after sunup and when I reached the hotel the three women were already in their wagon, waiting.

"Good morning, ladies," I greeted them cheerfully.

"Good morning," Kate Macklin replied, with no cheerfulness at all. I tipped my hat to the two girls, Sara and Billie. Billie lowered her eyes, but Sara gave me the full benefit of her blue ones.

"Look at them," Kate told me, indicating the street. People were lined up, as if for some great parade.

"Lined up to watch the last of the Macklins ride out of their town . . . and their lives."

"Can you blame them?" I asked.

She gave me a quick look, a sharp answer at the ready, but then she thought better of it and relaxed. "No," she answered, "I guess maybe I can't. Let's get going."

"Follow me," I told her.

I took the lead and we started towards the South end of town. I had mapped out the route in my head the night before, during the brief moments when Lizzie had let me be. I planned on following the Shawnee Trail from Missouri into Oklahoma, where we would shift over to the Chisholm Trail, which had been a very active cattle trail from 1867 to 1871, when it petered out. The Chisholm Trail would take us through to Texas, and then from there to Mexico.

With a few stops along the way for supplies, of course.

The three women were all seated on the seat of the buckboard, the rear of which was loaded with supplies. Trailing along behind, tied to the rear, were two extra horses. They could be substituted for the team now in use, or saddled and ridden that way.

Various remarks were thrown at the women as we road through town. I turned in the saddle once to see how they were taking it. Kate and Sara had their chins held up high, Billie's was customarily down on her chest.

When we were about twenty minutes out of town I slowed Duke down until I was riding alongside the buckboard.

"Are you all right?" I asked Kate.

"Why shouldn't we be?" she shot back.

"There were some pretty rough things said back there. I thought maybe you might have taken it to heart."

"What's it to you?" she demanded.

"Look, I thought that if we were going to be riding

together for a long period of time, we could try being friendly—or at least civil to each other."

"How friendly?" she asked suspiciously.

"Like you calling me Clint and my calling you ladies by your first names. We could start there, couldn't we?"

Kate looked over at Sara, who looked at me and then nodded to the older woman. That was no surprise. I knew Sara wouldn't mind getting friendly with me. I knew that since the first time we laid eyes on each other.

"All right . . . Clint," Kate told me. My name didn't exactly flow from her tongue like honey, but it was a start.

"Do you prefer Kate, Katy, or Katherine?" I asked her.

"I prefer Kate," she snapped, then as a small concession she added, "if you don't mind."

"Sara?" I said, leaning over and directing the same question to her.

"Sara's just fine," she assured me, smiling at me.

"What about Billie?"

"Her real name is Wilhemina, but we all call her Billie, so I guess you can, too," Kate told me.

"I think Wilhemina is a right pretty name," I told Billie, "but I'll call you Billie if you prefer."

"I-If you like," she replied.

"You're a smooth talker, Mist—I mean, Clint," Kate said to me.

"With a trio of ladies as lovely as you three, it comes easy," I assured her.

Shaking her head she gave me the first honest smile I'd seen since we met.

"Your smile is like a sunrise," I told her.

"Cut the crap," she told me, and setting the team into a trot left me momentarily behind. I shook my head, rode to catch up, then took the lead once again.

I remembered the word of Sam Hobson, about the

women not lasting ten minutes once they left town alone. I wondered how much more time we'd be given now that I was along. I kept my eyes and ears alert, but half an hour before dark I still hadn't seen any sign of anyone following us. We came upon a body of water too small to be called a lake and too large to be a stream, and I decided to camp right there.

"We've still got some daylight left," Kate protested.

"This is a good spot, and another twenty minutes travel is not going to find a better one," I told her. "We camp here."

"I'm in charge," she told me, "and I say we go on."

"I'm the guide and I say we camp here." She was about to go on arguing when I added, "Besides, I'm sure you and the girls wouldn't mind a bath, would you?"

We camped there.

I took care of the horses while the women had their baths. Kate was the first one finished and approached me while I was rubbing Duke down.

"He's a beautiful animal," she commented, patting his massive neck. I looked at her, with her hair dripping wet and her shirt sticking to her damp body, and avoided the obvious reply.

"Yes, he is," I said.

"What is he, five years old?"

"Just past that. I've had him since he was a yearling."

She bent over to inspect Duke a bit further and then asked, "Did you geld him?"

"Yes."

"How'd you like somebody to do that to you?" she asked, and then walked over by the fire I'd started.

The next one out was Billie. Her hair was as wet as her mother's was, but the fact that her shirt was also sticking to her body was not as readily noticeable. When she got closer, however, I could see the small mounds of her breasts topped by the little nubs of her nipples.

"Hi, Billie. How was the water?"
"It was fine."
"Hey, who does the cooking with you three?"
"I do."
"Well then, let's get to it. I'm starving."
She gave me a little smile and said, "Okay."
"Where's your sister?"
"She's, uh, around."
"She finished with her bath, too?"
"Yes."
"Good, I'm going to take a dip." I finished Duke off and put away his brush. "Tell your mother I'll be right along."
"Okay, Clint."

I gave Duke a parting pat as Billie walked away and told him, "Don't worry, boy, you ain't missing a thing." Then I thought about the night with Lizzie, but decided not to mention it to Duke. I didn't need a depressed gelding on my hands.

I went down to the water, dropped my clothes on a bush, set my gunbelt down on a rock and dove in.

I was splashing around for a couple of minutes, thinking about how only moments ago there were three lovely, naked women right where I was now, when all of a sudden I felt someone come up behind me. I felt arms go around my waist, and then two large, full, hard-tipped breasts pressed against my bare back.

"Sara?" I asked, only half-surprised.

"You're not surprised?" she asked, biting my ear from behind.

"I am, but I'm not. What would we tell your mother if she came back right now?"

"Why tell her anything?" she asked. "Why talk," she added, reaching down between my legs and tickling my scrotum. I squirmed a bit, a bit apprehensive about her mother or sister returning, but that finally faded. She swam around me and I closed my arms around her smooth, wet back and squeezed her tightly against me. Her nipples scraped my chest as I moved my hands down to her buttocks and pulled her crotch even tighter against mine. She imprisoned my erection between her thighs, and we stayed that way while I bore her back to shore. Once there I lowered her to the ground, half-in and half-out of the water. I took a moment to look at her. Her breasts, slick and smooth, looked like two marble slabs with pink cherries on top. She had much firmer breasts than Lizzie, and they stood almost straight out from her chest. I lowered myself beside her and tasted one nipple, and then the other.

"Harder," she told me, "bite them harder."

I did as she asked and she gasped and crushed my face against her marvelous breasts. I kissed them and bit them and then began to work my way down her body. She had the same clear white skin that Lizzie had, but Sara's belly was a flat slab. Her pubic hair was soft and fine and I rubbed my nose in it. She placed both her hands behind my head and pushed my face deep into her crotch. I used my tongue to locate her most sensitive part and then grabbed it with my teeth.

"Suck it," she pleaded. "Suck it hard!"

I did just that and she began to writhe beneath me. The water came up from between her thighs and mingled with her own wetness. I alternated between sucking on her and pushing my tongue deep inside of her and she gasped and whispered, "Again, again . . ."

Finally I worked my way back up her magnificent body until I reached her mouth. I kissed her hard enough to bruise her lips and she reached down between us for my penis and guided it home.

"Oh, yes . . ." she sighed. "Do it, Clint, do it hard! I love it hard!"

I did it as hard as I could and it seemed to satisfy her.

She came twice in quick succession, and then the third time I went with her. By the time we were done we had dug a small trench in the wet dirt.

We went for a swim afterward, to clean up, and then returned to shore. She pressed herself tightly against me and put her arms around my neck.

"Now we know each other much better," she told me. Our lips met again and our tongues intertwined . . . and then there was a scream.

"That's Billie," she told me, her eyes frightened.

"Stay here," I told her. I grabbed my gun and ran back toward the camp with my pants in the other hand.

It was almost dark and in the light from the fire I saw Kate and Billie struggling with three men. One man was holding Billie, the second had Kate, and the other was watching the trees . . . for me, I assumed, or at least for Sara.

Then I recognized the man holding Kate. He had one hand around her neck and the other was cupping one of her large breasts.

It was Shagan.

The man holding Billie had his hand inside her shirt. "They're tiny," he was saying, "but they feel good."

I almost called out to them, but I could see where that would lead. The women would become shields, and I'd be forced to give up my gun. One minute after that happened, we'd all be dead.

I made some time to think in by putting on my pants, keeping my eyes on what was going on inside the camp. At that moment Sara came up beside me, fully dressed.

"We've got to do something," she told me, pulling on my arm.

"Take it easy," I told her, "and keep your voice down. If we go rushing in there, they'll only hide behind your mother and sister. There's another way."

"What?"

I tried to think and I looked at Sara while I was doing it. Her shirt was plastered to her body the way her mother's had been, outlining every contour, including her nipples, which were still distended. Her hair was soaked and lying flat against her head.

"I've got an idea," I told her.

"What is it?"

"Your mother and sister are beautiful, Sara, but physically, you're incredible."

"Clint, this is not time for sweet talk," she admonished me.

"I know that, Sara. Listen, I want you to walk into that camp."

"Sure, that'll give the third man somebody to hide behind," she said, sarcastically.

"Sara, trust me. I want you to walk into camp like you don't see those men. Be wringing out your hair, or something."

She looked at me funny and asked, "Are you crazy?"

"And have your shirt open."

She nodded to herself and answered her own question. "You are crazy."

"Wide open. They'll be so busy looking at you coming into camp at that end, that they won't see me coming in at this end," I told her, pointing first to one end and then the other.

She thought about it a moment, then said, "Well, if that's the best you can come up with, I guess it'll have to do."

She started away, then turned back and asked, "Are you sure you're good with that gun?"

"Sara, after all we've been to each other, would I lie to you?" I asked.

"You're a man, aren't you?" she answered, and then ran off to circle the camp and come in from the other side.

Kate and Billie were putting up a pretty good struggle. I heard Shagan tell Kate, "All we want's a little fun, bitch . . . and Macklin's treasure."

At that point Kate kicked backwards and caught Shagan on the shin. He started howling and hopping around, the way he had been in the saloon, and Kate ran for the wagon. Suddenly Sara came strolling into camp, and I had to give her credit. She probably felt more like running, but in she came, walking slowly, head tilted to one side as she squeezed water from her hair. Her shirt was open and with her head tilted that way, the shirt hung wide open, exposing totally one magnificently rounded breast.

"Jesus, Shagan, look at that!" one of the men shouted in awe. Shagan stopped hopping around to stare hungrily at Sara. The man holding Billie let her go in order to stare at Sara's near nakedness. Billie ran over to where Kate was standing by the wagon. From there they also stared at Sara's entrance.

I made my move.

"Don't anybody move," I ordered, stepping from the brush.

"Shit!" Shagan snapped. The other two men alternated their eyes between Sara and me, and that slowed down their reactions.

"Keep your hands away from your guns," I shouted, and almost simultaneously Shagan yelled, "Spread out!" and went for his gun.

"Don't!" I yelled.

It all happened too quick for me to even be sure I remember it correctly. I'm pretty sure I took out the man on the left first, since he was the closest one to me. By that time Shagan and the other man had their guns out. Had I been armed with a single-action Colt, rather than my modified double-action, they might have got me. Instead, I squeezed off three quick ones, two going into Shagan's chest and the third one killing the third man.

By the time the action slowed down, there were three dead men, and none of them were me. I admired the three women, as I hadn't heard one scream during the shooting, but then being Con Macklin's women, I guess they were used to shooting.

I walked to the fallen men and checked to make sure they were all dead. Then I turned to the three women and said, "I'll get rid of them." To Sara I added, "Button up and have dinner ready when I get back."

7

I found the dead men's horses not far from camp. I unsaddled them and let them go, then disposed of the saddles and their owners.

When I returned to camp I could smell the bacon cooking. I had retrieved the remainder of my clothes and was fully dressed. While dressing I thought about what had happened between Sara and me. Would it happen again during the trip? I had no doubt but that it would. If she weren't the one to make it happen a second time, I would be.

When I approached the fire Billie handed me a tin pan filled with bacon, beans, and bread. I sat down next to Kate and proceeded to eat it. Sara was on the other side of the fire and her eyes met mine without any expression crossing her face.

"What did you do with them?" Kate asked.

"You really want to know?" I asked her. I scooped up some beans with a hunk of bread and popped it into my mouth. I followed that with a hunk of bacon.

"Yes, I do," she told me firmly.

"I weighed them down with their saddles and threw them into the stream," I told her. "Then I let their horses go." It was a bit backwards, but that didn't matter.

"What about their gear?"

"Sank that, too."

"Did you at least take their money before you dumped them?"

I looked at her for a long moment, then told her, "I don't rob the dead, Mrs. Macklin. If you wanted their money then you should have disposed of their bodies yourself." With that I got up and took my plate over to the wagon. I sat with my back against a wheel and continued to eat.

I was almost finished and ready for more when Sara approached, carrying another plate and a cup of coffee. She sat down next to me and handed me the plate.

"For you," she told me. "I figure you worked up a pretty good appetite today."

"You figure right," I told her, taking the food gratefully. "That mine, too?" I asked, indicating the coffee.

"That," she said, indicating the plate in my hand, "this," lifting the cup higher, "and anything else I have."

"The coffee will do for now," I told her, taking it from her. She placed her hands on her knees but made no move to get up.

"You have to forgive Momma," she told me.

"Do I?"

"About the money, I mean. She's had a hard life, had to scrounge for everything she ever got—"

"Old habits die hard, you mean?"

"—until she met Con Macklin," she finished.

"Macklin? Is that what you call your father?"

"Oh, he's not my father."

"Billie's?"

"No, not hers, either. Our father died years ago, but Macklin was good to us, like we were his."

I cleaned the plate with the last of the bread and then

drank the last of the coffee.

"Another cup?" she asked.

"Thanks," I said, handing her the empty. She went to the fire, poured another cup and had an exchange of words with Kate, then returned.

"Momma thinks I've got my eye on you," she told me, handing me the full cup.

"What did you tell her?"

She smiled at me and answered, "I told her that maybe I did."

"Why?"

"Why what?"

"Why would you—I mean, why did you—"

"Why did I force myself on you?"

I smiled at her and said, "Well, it wasn't exactly by force, Sara, but that's the general idea."

She shrugged.

"You appeal to me, Clint. When a man appeals to me, I let him know. I've done it before and I'll probably do it again. You were better than most, by the way."

"Thanks," I said, wryly.

"That doesn't mean I love you, or anything," she cautioned me.

"Of course not."

She nodded to herself, saying, "I knew you were like me."

"How's that?"

"You like it wherever and whenever you can get it," she told me boldly.

I stared at her a few moments, took a sip of my second cup of coffee, then told her, "I guess that's fair—within reason."

"We have a long way to go," she told me. "I know we can find another opportunity."

"Maybe we'll even make one," I proposed.

She tilted her head and replied, "Maybe we will at that."

"Tell me something."

"What?"

"You and Kate sound like you've had some education, maybe in the east."

"Well, so do you."

"I have," I told her. "I spent most of my youth in the east, but what about you?"

"We've had some," she confirmed. "Billie hasn't been as lucky as I have, but she's smart as a whip. I'm teachin' her to read and write some."

"That's good."

"How come you can shoot that fast without fannin' your gun?" she asked, changing the subject. "Momma has a big Colt that Macklin gave her, but she has to cock the hammer before she can fire it."

"I modified mine myself," I told her, taking it from my holster. I explained how I went about taking a single action gun and converting it to a double-action or self-cocking revolver.

"Can I see it?" she asked.

"Sure," I told her. I unloaded the gun and handed it to her.

"How do you clean it?" she asked. "It's solid. How can you break it down?" she added, handing it back.

"Basically, it's a Colt," I told her. "A couple of men in England invented some improvements, like a solid body design and the double-action feature. It hasn't caught on over here, but I heard about it and decided to try it."

"Are you a gunsmith by trade?"

"That's right. Anyway, I tried it with a few guns and eventually came up with this. I still cock it to fire accurately. The double-action increases the speed, but cuts down on the accuracy because it requires more pressure to pull the trigger and that can throw off your aim." I reloaded the gun and replaced it in my holster. I get over enthusiastic when I'm talking about guns, sometimes.

"Have you ever been to England?" she asked, developing a dreamy look in her eyes.

"No, never. I'd like to, though. They seem to have some pretty advanced ideas about guns over there."

"Never mind the guns," she told me, "I'd like to see the sights. I'll get over there one of these days," she said with great determination. "I'll travel a lot, wait and see."

"I don't doubt it," I told her. With her talents, she'd get some man to take her there, sooner or later.

"Why don't you go back and sit with Kate and Billie," I suggested. She looked surprised until I added, "I want to go over tomorrow's route, and I can't concentrate with you so close."

"Momma's right about you, Clint."

"In what way?"

"You are a smooth talker," she told me, getting to her feet. Before leaving, however, she leaned over, giving me the opportunity to glance down her shirt front, and added, "but I like it."

8

Kate set up the sleeping arrangements: the three of them on one side of the wagon, me on the other side, and blankets hanging from both sides. I guess she figured that removed temptation from my mind.

Once we all said goodnight I settled down to clean my gun, and reviewed the events of the day, including my time with Sara. After reliving those glorious minutes with her, I wondered if Shagan and his two partners had come out after us on their own, or if someone had put them up to it—like Dade Whitman.

I had strong doubts about Dade Whitman's story concerning Con Macklin. The townspeople of Baxterville may have bought it, but that was because they'd have bought anything that would rid them of Con Macklin, and also they didn't know Whitman the way I did. I wouldn't put it past Whitman to have worked something out with Macklin, and then staged the whole business of chasing Macklin down and killing him.

And yes, that meant that I didn't necessarily believe that Macklin was dead. For all I knew, I was guiding these women to meet with him in Mexico.

However, even if Whitman and Macklin had worked a deal, I couldn't see Macklin turning over his so-called treasure to Dade. For that reason I suspected Dade

Whitman of having sent Shagan and his partners to ambush us and find Macklin's treasure. That meant that Whitman must have had something on Shagan to be able to trust him to come back with the information, or the treasure.

Either that, or Shagan was just plain afraid of Whitman, which was not at all unlikely.

I finished cleaning the gun and reloaded it. I set out my bedroll, put the gun where I could reach it easily, and then lay down on my back. There was a large star up in the sky that reminded me of the star I used to wear on my chest. I'd worn one since I was twenty-two, and after sixteen years had decided to take it off. That had been six months ago, and I was still wondering if I had done the right thing. Being a lawman wasn't what it used to be. There wasn't much respect for the law anymore, and I had gotten tired of that attitude and decided to pack it in. I used the money I'd saved to buy my team and wagon, and some new equipment, and decided just to travel around, minding my own business, making some money here and there by gunsmithing or selling guns.

And here I was, involved in someone else's business, and I'd already had to kill three men.

I tried to relax and make my mind a blank while staring at that one big star in the sky. I half-expected Sara to take the chance and come around the wagon when Kate and Billie fell asleep, but she didn't come, and pretty soon I fell asleep.

We were three days out of Baxterville, and three days into Oklahoma and still there had been no further ambush attempts. I was about ready to break us off the Shawnee Trail to the Chisholm Trail. Once we picked up the Chisholm Trail I planned to stop in a little town called Anadarko for supplies. Once we restocked we'd travel the Trail through Oklahoma—hopefully without encountering any Shawnee raiding parties—into Texas, and then on to Mexico.

I had decided to leave the three women behind when I went into Anadarko. There was no sense in looking for trouble by taking three beautiful women into town with me and dangling them in front of every cowpoke and hardcase. I remembered what Sara said about Kate having a big Colt, and figured they'd be all right until I got back.

Speaking of Sara, we still hadn't had an opportunity to enjoy each other's company again, but Kate started noticing the looks that passed between us. I wasn't too sure whether or not Billie had. Every time I looked at her, she seemed to be looking at the ground.

The night before I intended to start for town Kate brought her dinner over by me.

"I know something's going on between you and Sara," she told me, coming right to the point.

"How do you know that?" I asked.

"She didn't tell me, and neither will you, but I see the way you look at each other. She's still very young, you know," she reminded me. "I know I'm the one who told you she looks older, and at times she even acts older, but she is only eighteen."

"Why are you telling me all this?" I asked.

"I just want you to know, that's all," she answered. "She's young and vulnerable. Don't hurt her."

"I have no intention of hurting her, Kate. I think she may even be a little older than you realize. Have you spoken to her about this?"

"Not the way I'm talking to you right now."

"Try it," I suggested. "Try talking to her woman-to-woman and see what happens. You may be surprised."

She compressed her lips and changed the subject.

"When are we going into Anadarko?" she asked.

I set my empty plate and cup down beside me and said, "I've decided to ride in alone tomorrow. There's no use in looking for trouble by taking you three along. It's a pretty raw town and bringing you three into it would be doing just that. You should all be pretty safe here until I get back."

"I'll come with you," she said firmly.

"Why? Do you think I'm going to run out on you? Do you think I'll be satisfied with only half of the money I'm owed?"

"That's not it at all. With me along perhaps you won't be so tempted to have that extra drink, or sit down at a card table. We'll go into town, buy the supplies, and come right back."

"If I left you behind it would be just like you to saddle up and ride after me anyway, wouldn't it?" I asked her.

"Yes, it would."

I sighed. "Then you might as well come along. Will the girls be all right alone?" I asked.

"I told you," she said, rising and gathering up the empties, "in some ways she's much older than eighteen. But only in some ways, Clint."

9

In the morning I saddled Duke and one of the extra horses. The second horse we brought with us to carry the supplies.

"You're sure the girls will be all right?" I asked Kate before we left.

"They'll be fine. I've left Sara my Colt, and Billie knows how to use the rifle. I told them we'd be back tonight, or tomorrow morning, at the latest."

I looked at her, wondering why she would think we'd have to stay in town overnight, but she was looking straight ahead, with no expression on her face.

"I guess we'd better get started, then."

We both waved to Sara and Billie, and I noticed a curious look on Sara's face. She was upset about something, and I didn't know if it was the fact that she and Billie were being left behind, or that Kate was coming with me.

It was a two-hour ride into Anadarko and we made it in relative silence. Kate was dressed in jeans and a plaid shirt, with high boots and a neckerchief. Her red hair fell around her shoulders, and it shone brightly when the sun hit it. I examined her profile and found that, curiously, neither one of the girls looked anything like her. In fact, they didn't even look like each other. It was also curious that she was red-haired, Billie was dark and Sara was blonde.

When we got to town we tied up the horses in front of the General Store.

"I want to make a stop before we go in," she told me. "Why don't you go over to the saloon and wait for me."

That surprised me. Last night one of her reasons for coming with me had been to make sure I didn't go on a binge and forget to come back. Now she was suggesting I go have a drink.

"All right, Kate. Take your time," I told her.

I went over to the saloon and ordered a beer. It was afternoon, and Anadarko was not at all like Baxterville. It was larger, and rougher, and at any time of day you'd find a good number of cowpokes and hardcases hanging around the saloon, drinking and playing poker. While I was on my first beer a dispute over a poker hand erupted, and escalated into a fight. There was no gunplay, but the bartender got involved, and the participants were delivered out into the street, where they could settle their differences without causing any property damage.

When the bartender came back I ordered another beer and said, "Is that an everyday occurrence?"

"It sure is, and with those same cowpokes, too. They're the best of friends."

"It simplifies matters afterward," I told him, and he agreed.

I wondered where Kate had gone off to, and then an idea struck me.

"Do you have a telegraph office in town?" I asked him.

"Just down the street a ways," he told me. "Got an important message to send?"

"Nothing that would keep me from having one more beer," I answered.

"Just get into town?" he asked when he brought me the beer.

"That's right. Picking up some supplies."

"Then you haven't heard the news."

"What news is that?"

"Wild Bill's in town," he told me, his face reflecting the awe he felt.

"Bill's in town?" I repeated.

"Shore is. They say he quit marshallin' up Abilene way and he's just travelin' the Chisholm Trail."

I hadn't seen Bill for some years, and it was ironic that we'd end up in the same town on the Chisholm Trail, both having given up our stars.

"Has he been in here yet?" I asked.

"Nope, not yet, but I'm hopin'."

"Don't worry," I told him, "he won't stay away from here for long. You've got the three things Bill loves best."

"What might that be?"

"Liquor, cards, and girls," I told him, indicating all three in turn. Compared to the ladies I was traveling with, the saloon girls were second-rate, but they were available.

"You sound like you know Wild Bill," the bartender said.

"We've been known to drink out of the same bottle from time to time," I admitted.

Now that I knew Bill was in town I didn't want to leave without seeing him. I also knew I wouldn't be able to find Bill unless he wanted to be found, so I'd have to sit and wait for him to come to me.

But first I'd have to see Kate.

"I'll be back," I told the bartender, slapping some money down on the bar.

When I left the saloon I saw her waiting in front of the General Store. She must have finished with her other business, and was waiting for me to buy the supplies with her.

I crossed the street and when I reached her she asked, "You're not drunk, are you?"

"Not yet," I told her. I walked past her into the store, and she followed. We picked out the supplies that we needed, and when I paid I gave the clerk an extra couple of dollars and asked him if he'd see that the stuff was loaded onto my pack horse.

"Why can't you do it?" she asked.

"I just found out that an old friend is in town. I don't want to leave without seein' him."

"What am I supposed to do in the meantime?" she demanded.

"I don't care. Do some shopping, or you can wait with me in the saloon."

"The saloon?"

"My friend will show up there sooner or later."

"And if you're not drunk when he does, you will be after. I'd better come along, just to keep you honest."

"Are all men drunks to you?" I asked her.

"All but Macklin," she answered, then hurriedly added, "while he was alive."

"C'mon," I told her, "I'll buy you a drink."

We went to the saloon and took a back table. Kate attracted a lot of attention. Even dressed in mannish clothes, with trail dust on her, she outshone the painted saloon girls. I got two beers from the bar and carried them to the table.

"What's your friend look like?" she asked.

"You'll know him when he comes in," I assured her. "The place will go quiet, and then you'll hear people start mumbling. When he sits down things'll get back to normal."

She laughed. "Who is he, God?"

"Some people think so."

It was a few hours before Bill walked in, but someone else walked in who caught my attention. He wasn't very old, about twenty-three or so, kind of tall and thin. He wore his gun strapped down and low on his hip, a vest and a flat-rimmed, black hat. He ordered a drink at the bar, then paid for the bottle and took it to a table. He looked kind of sad, and seemed bent on drinking himself into a stupor.

I was buzzing a little, and Kate's head was on a little crooked, too, when trouble walked in. Six hardcases walked in together, with no pretext of being anything but six men looking for trouble.

"Kate."

"Yeah?"

"When I tell you—and not before—I want you to back into the corner and get down. Do you hear me?"

She wasn't so far gone that she didn't realize something was wrong. Her eyes cleared a bit and she asked, "What's wrong, Clint?"

"I think we've got more company," I told her.

"How can you tell?"

"I can feel it. Just be ready to move when I tell you."

I could feel it, all right, like something solid in the air. Four of the men went to the bar and ordered drinks, two stayed by the door. I kept my eye on them until one of the ones at the bar nodded to one of them at the door. I loosed my gun in my holster as the two by the door approached the table.

"Hey, Red, how's about some fun with a couple of men?" one of them asked.

"Fine," Kate told them. "Find me a couple and we'll see what we can do."

That got a laugh from the others in the saloon, but the man who had spoken turned red.

I thought I had it figured. They'd pick a fight with me over Kate, kill me and take her. Then they'd try to get her to tell where Macklin's treasure was.

"Don't get smart, bitch."

"The lady was just speaking her mind, cowboy. Why don't you go over by the bar with your friends and forget it," I suggested.

"I ain't gonna forget nothin', Mister. Me and my friends wanta borrow your girl for a spell. Whataya say?"

"I said back off, friend, and I'm not going to say it again."

"We'll back off," he told me. He and the second man did just that. They backed up until they were standing at the bar with the other four.

"You better stand up, Mister," the one doing the talking said. "You don't wanna buy it sittin' down."

"Kate," I said, "move into the corner. Keep down."

"Clint—"

"Do what I tell you," I snapped. I waited until she had moved behind me, then I stood up. Six against one. Even with my double-action gun I couldn't hope to get them before they got me.

Then I heard a voice off to the side, a little slurred, but still understandable.

"Six against one seems a little uneven, don't it, boys?" the voice asked. There was a flurry of activity as the rest of the patrons of the saloon headed for cover. I turned my head and saw the young guy with the flat-rimmed hat standing up, his right hand dangling by his gun.

"You're buying yourself trouble that isn't yours, son," I told him.

"I'm makin' it mine, Mister. I don't stand by and watch six men gun down one man."

"So we'll gun down two," the man by the bar said. "It don't make much difference to us either way."

"Better make it three, friend," another voice said. "And I think we just called your hand, and raised it."

I looked by the front door, and there was Bill, a gun on each hip, and his hands itching to grab them.

"It's Wild Bill," one of the men at the bar whispered, and a few of them started looking around and wetting their lips.

"I didn't sign on to draw against Wild Bill," another one said.

"Shut up," the one doing most of the talking said. "It's too late, now."

"Your friend's right," Bill agreed. "It's too late to do anything but go for your guns, friends."

I heard Kate catch her breath behind me and slide to the floor, and then the six men at the bar moved.

It was an even split. I took the two on my right before their guns cleared their holsters. The tall kid gunned the two in the middle almost before their hands could move, and Bill finished up the two on the left, teasing them a little by letting them touch their guns and dying happy, knowing they got that far against Wild Bill.

Bill and I checked the six of them to make sure they were dead, while the kid sat back down and drained what was left of his bottle.

We leaned against the bar and Bill told the bartender —who had ducked down under the bar during the shooting—"Whiskey, two bottles."

To me he said, "Clint, it's good to see you again," and we shook hands.

"I don't think I was ever happier to see you, Bill," I told him, honestly.

"Who were your friends?" he asked.

"Messenger boys," I told him, positive that they had been sent by Dade Whitman.

Bill poured himself a drink, and one for me. He was a tall man wearing a gambler's suit, which is what he was when he wasn't a lawman or, as some people called him, a gunman. His hair was longer than I remembered, and he had a long mustache. He was about four years younger than me, but he looked older.

"Who's our other friend?" he asked, indicating the tall youth who was now staring at his empty bottle.

"I don't know. Why don't we bring him a drink and ask him," I suggested.

"Good idea."

We each grabbed a bottle and we walked over to the youth's table, and sat.

"You look like you could use a drink, friend," I told him.

His eyes brightened when he saw the bottle and he said, "I do believe you are right, frien'," and he held out his glass. I filled it and he emptied it.

"Refill?" he asked.

"Why not?" Bill answered, and gave it to him from the other bottle.

"My name's—" Bill began to introduce himself, but the kid stopped him.

"I know who you are, Bill," he said, "and it was a pleasure to side with you."

"Well, it was my friend here that we was sidin' with," Bill told him. "This here's Clint Adams. Clint and I were lawmen together a ways back. Folks got to callin' him 'The Gunsmith' back then."

The young fellow looked at me and said, "Seems I've heard tell some stories about you, too. Glad to be of help."

"I'm glad you were here . . ." I said, fishing for his name.

"Name's Earp," he told me, not offering a first name.

"Where're you from, young Mr. Earp?" Bill asked.

"Did some lawman work up in Lamar, Missouri for a while," he told us. "My wife died a while back, took sick with typhoid, and I guess I caught the wanderlust after that."

"Headin' anywhere special?" Bill asked.

"No. Figured on headin' South for a while, but lately I been thinkin' 'bout headin' North, to Kansas."

"I jest come from Kansas," Bill told us.

"I heard you quit marshalling up in Abilene, Bill," I remarked.

"Yeah, did it for 'bout eight months or so, but figured it was time to move on."

"I'm mighty glad you moved in this direction," I told him.

"You still wearin' a star?" he asked.

"No, I gave mine up six months ago."

"Hell, here we are, three ex-lawmen sittin' in a saloon with six dead men—and one lovely lady," he added, looking behind me.

I turned around and saw that Kate had taken her seat at the table we had been sitting at, and was staring at us like we each had two heads.

"Guess she's wonderin' how we could be socializin' after we each jest gunned down two men," Bill observed.

"She's used to gunplay," I told him.

"She yourn?" he asked.

"Nope. I'm just escorting her and her daughters to Mexico. They had some trouble in Missouri."

"Where abouts?" Earp asked.

"Baxterville, or what used to be called Macklinville."

"Used to be?" he asked. "Macklin left that town?"

"Not on his own." I explained the circumstances, and Bill's eyes lit up when he heard about Dade Whitman.

"That's a bad man," he told me. "I don't know if that town made out so good in the exchange."

"I agree."

At that point the sheriff of Anadarko put in an appearance with a couple of deputies.

"What's goin' on here?" he demanded. "What's all the shootin'?"

"It was a fair fight, Sheriff," the bartender told him. "Wild Bill and these other two fellers had no choice."

"Wild Bill, huh?" the sheriff said, turning to face us.

"Sheriff," Bill said, raising his glass.

"We don't need no trouble in this town, Bill," the sheriff told him, trying not to be awed by Bill's presence. The two young deputies with him did not have that problem. They were openly impressed with Bill.

"No trouble on my part, Sheriff. I was jest backin' my friend, here," Bill said, pointing to me.

"And what might your name be?" he asked me.

"Clint Adams."

"What's your business in town, Mr. Adams?"

"Just picking up some supplies."

"Well, I'll need statements from all of you before you leave town. The morning will do. For now, I'll have to get rid of these bodies." He turned to his deputies and told them, "Get some men from outside to help you move these bodies."

He turned back to us, then looked at Kate.

"Was the lady involved?" he asked me.

"She's with me," I answered, hoping that would satisfy him.

"What about this young feller?"

"I'll make a statement 'fore I leave town," Earp promised.

"Good 'nough," the Sheriff said, and then supervised the removal of the dead men.

"Well, I guess I better see about a couple of hotel rooms," I said, rising from my seat.

"I'll stay and get acquainted with our new friend, here. We seem to have some things in common."

"See you in the morning, then." I passed young Earp my bottle and said, "See if you can drink this old lawman under the table, youngster," I told him.

He took the bottle from me and said, "I'll do my best."

I walked over to Kate and asked her, "Are you all right?"

"Yes, I—I think so. I'm just—that all happened so fast, I—is that Wild Bill—"

"Yes, it is. He's the friend I was waiting for," I explained.

"He got here just in time, didn't he? What about the boy?"

"He's a new friend. His name is Earp. That's all I know about him. C'mon, Kate, we're going to have to get hotel rooms."

"Why?"

"I have to stay until morning, to make a statement at the sheriff's office."

She looked at me for a few moments, then got up and said, "I guess the girls will be all right overnight, and I am a bit shaky."

That surprised me. I had expected her to argue, but she'd given in very easily—too easily.

I waved to Bill and Earp as we left and we went over to the hotel.

"Got two rooms?" I asked the clerk.

"Yeah," he answered, and turned his back to find two keys.

"On the same floor, please," Kate told him. He had taken two keys down, and when she spoke he replaced one and removed another one.

"Here you are," he said, handing us the keys. We both signed the register. "Any luggage?"

"None. We hadn't intended to stay overnight."

"Where can I get a bath?" Kate asked.

"If you go down the back stairs from your floor and out the back door, we have some bath facilities there," the man told her. He was a little man with an Eastern accent and Eastern clothes. I wondered what he was doing in Anadarko, but didn't dwell on the question.

"Thanks," I told him, and we went up. We'd had to wait for Bill a pretty long while, but would still have had time to ride back to camp had it not been for the shooting incident. Now it was pretty late and I was ready to turn in, just to bring tomorrow on a little faster.

"I'll see you in the morning, Kate," I told her when we reached her door.

"I'm going to get a bath and then go to sleep. See you tomorrow—early. I don't want to delay any longer than we have to."

"I agree. Goodnight."

"Goodnight . . . Clint."

10

I could hear Kate moving around in her room, before and after her bath. Against my better judgment I began to visualize her naked, with beads of water running down her breasts and thighs. That was enough to keep me from sleeping, no matter how tired I was. I also started to wonder how she would compare in the nude to Sara.

Thoughts of Sara and Kate ruined any chance I may have had of sleep altogether.

I was looking out the window, smoking a cigarette, when there was a knock on my door.

"Who is it?" I asked from the window.

"Kate," came the reply from behind the door.

"Come on in. It's unlocked."

She walked in and closed the door behind her—and locked it. She was dressed, but I could smell the fresh, clean scent of her across the room.

"What is it, Kate?" I asked. "Couldn't you sleep?"

"No, I couldn't," she said, hugging her arms as if she were cold. "What about you?"

"Uh, no, I couldn't sleep, either," I admitted, although I didn't tell her the reason.

"Were you thinking about Sara?"

I looked at her in surprise.

"Or of me, right in the next room?"

I watched her as she started to unbutton her shirt.

"I was thinking about you, Clint," she told me, peeling the shirt from her damp skin to reveal beautifully rounded, firm breasts. Her hands moved to her belt as she said, "That's why I haven't been able to sleep. I need a man, Clint," she went on, removing her pants. She had obviously dressed without undergarments, and I hadn't noticed that she was barefoot. As a result, she was now totally invitingly naked.

"I need you, Clint," she said, holding her arms out to me.

She was shorter than Sara, and her figure was not quite as full, but when I gathered her up in my arms, she felt just as delightful.

I put her on the bed and started exploring her body with my tongue. I started with her breasts, sucking on her nipples until they were hard as little rocks, then worked my way down her body, going down her thighs and legs, all the way to her ankles, and then back up again. When I turned my concentration to the core of her womanhood, she began to buck beneath me, crying out, "I'm on fire, I'm on fire . . ."

I worked on her until she reached a shattering orgasm, and then kept it up until I thought my tongue would fall out. At that point I moved up on the bed and began to tease her by touching her wetness with my erection, but never quite penetrating.

"Don't make me beg," she said in my ear. "Do it, do it, don't make me beg."

I was tempted to go ahead and make her beg, but the truth was that I couldn't wait either. I rammed it home, and her legs came up around me, holding me tightly inside of her. Our movements were frenzied and uncoordinated, but eventually we found the tempo and began to move together.

"Oh, God," she yelled as she came for the second time, nails raking at my back, pulling at my buttocks, trying to force me yet deeper.

I was still unfulfilled and kept up the tempo until she came again. Finally, I felt the great rush build up inside of me, and I let go into her hot, moist tunnel.

"Oh, God, I needed that," she said afterward as we lay side by side.

"Think you'll be able to sleep now?" I asked her.

"No," she said, touching my limp penis, "not just yet."

One thing that Kate had on Sara was experience, and it showed as she used her mouth and began to work on me. She found places to put her tongue that I never even knew existed, and when she was done my erection was harder than before. She held herself above me and then lowered herself, impaling herself on my pole. I watched her as she rode up and down on me, her face reflecting the pleasure she felt, her full breasts bouncing beautifully. When she felt that I was about to come she said, "Not yet, Clint, not yet, please."

I gritted my teeth and held on as long as I could, until she told me in short gasps, "Okay . . . now . . . now . . . now!"

She drummed her heels against my buttocks as we both came together and when it was over I felt her relax her muscles and release the breath she was holding.

"You know what?" she asked in my ear.

"What?"

"I think I can sleep now."

We both did.

11

The next morning I met up with Wild Bill and the young Mr. Earp and we went to the Sheriff's office to give out statements.

When I woke up, Kate was gone, and when we met for breakfast, she was the Kate of old again, and not the passionate woman who had spent the night in my bed. When Bill and Earp came in, she told me she'd be waiting in her room and when I was ready to leave, so was she.

"That's a mighty good-lookin' woman," Bill told me as we walked to the sheriff's office.

"Yeah," I answered.

"You sure she ain't yours?"

I thought about the previous night, but the answer still had to be the same. "No, she's not mine."

We made our statements and they matched that of the saloon's bartender, so there were no problems about any of us leaving town.

Outside the sheriff's office we said our farewells.

"Headed for Mexico, Clint?" Bill asked.

"That's where I'm being paid to go," I told him. "What about you?"

He shrugged, saying, "Just ridin'. Thought I might

leave town with young Mr. Earp, here, and see where we end up."

I shook hands with him and said, "It was good seeing you again, Bill."

"Stay out of trouble," he advised.

"It was good meeting you," I told Earp, taking his hand. "Especially under those circumstances."

"It was my pleasure," he assured me. "Maybe we'll meet up with each other again, some time."

"I hope so," I told him.

They had their horses ready and I watched them mount up and ride out of town. In between the Saloon and hotel last night, we had put up our horses and supplies at the livery stable, so I went and got them and brought them around to the front of the hotel before I called Kate from her room.

"Time to go," I told her.

She nodded and shut the door behind her. Without a word she went down ahead of me, mounted her horse and started out of town. I took the lead rope of the supply horse and followed her.

About ten minutes out I called to her to stop and rode up beside her.

"You want to talk about it?" I asked.

She shook her head.

"Kate, it was a need, that's all. We both needed it and it's nothing to be ashamed of."

"I don't want to walk about it," she insisted.

I shrugged and said, "Okay, fine. Let's go."

When we got back to the camp the girls were preparing something to eat. You didn't normally stop on the trail for lunch, but since we were already camped, they decided to have it waiting for us.

Kate dismounted and went to change her clothes without speaking to me.

"What happened?" Sara asked. "You're late."

"We ran into a little difficulty," I told her, and explained about everything that had happened.

"It looks like they're not gonna leave us alone," she observed.

"They're after Macklin's treasure—whatever that is."

Although I hadn't phrased it as a question, she recognized it as one.

"I don't know what it is, Clint—or if there even is one. Only Kate would know that. Right, Billie?"

Billie looked up, avoided my eyes, and said, "That's right."

"There's one thing I wonder about," I told the girls.

"What's that?"

"How'd they know that we would be in Anadarko? How did Whitman know to send six men there after us?"

"Maybe he figured out which route you'd take to Mexico," she suggested.

"And figured that I'd pick Anadarko as the place to replenish our supplies?" I shook my head. "I can't buy that. There are too many possible routes to take for him to hit it right on the head like that."

"Maybe he covered them all," she suggested further.

"That's possible, but it would take an awful lot of men."

"You've killed nine already. Who knows how many more he may have?"

She certainly had a lot of suggestions. I decided not to listen to any more of them, before she had me convinced that behind every tree was a man with a gun.

"What's for lunch?" I asked.

"The last of everything," she told me.

"Not anymore," I assured her, and began to unload the supplies we'd brought from town.

By the time I was done—no help offered from any of

the ladies, naturally—the food was ready. Kate chose to sit by the wagon with Sara, which left me to have lunch with Billie, the lady with whom I'd had the least contact —in more ways than one.

"How was it while we were gone?" I asked her, just to make conversation.

"Fine."

"No problems, no trouble?"

"No."

"You know, Sara told me she was teaching you how to read and write, is that right?"

"Yes."

"Did she teach you how to make a sentence yet?"

"What?" she asked, not understanding what I meant.

"That's what I mean," I told her. "I've been making conversation, and you've been perfecting one word sentences."

She looked sheepish and said, "I'm sorry."

"That's better, at least it was two words."

"Oh . . ."

"All right, we'll call a truce. You don't have to talk if you don't want to," I offered.

"I don't mind."

"Good."

"Was that true?"

"What?"

"About you knowing those men. I mean, Wild Bill—"

"Bill and I are old friends, yes."

"That's exciting," she said, her eyes sparkling.

"Well, Bill's an exciting man, although he may not think so. He really can't see what all the fuss is about."

"Is he faster than you? With a gun, I mean."

"Bill? He's faster than God. With a gun, I mean."

She laughed, a little girl's laugh, although she really

wasn't a little girl. At sixteen she was nearly a woman, and a damned good-looking one, at that. Especially those eyes.

"Did you get those eyes from your father?" I asked.

"My eyes?"

"Yes. They're not your mother's," I said, pointing to Kate. "Hers are green. Were your father's brown?"

"Y-yes," she answered, a little nervously, I thought.

"I wonder why Sara's are blue?"

She shrugged and mumbled, "I don't know. I gotta clean my plate," she added, and got up and scurried away.

It looked like questions about her parentage made her uncomfortable, or scared her. I looked over at Sara and Kate and they were deep in conversation, during which they would occasionally glance my way. I finished what was left in my plate, then left it on the ground and walked over to where they sat. When they saw me coming, they discontinued their conversation.

"Well, ladies?" I said.

"Well what?" Kate asked.

"Are we going on?"

"Of course we're going on. Why wouldn't we?" she demanded.

"Maybe because of what happened in Anadarko," I suggested.

The flash in her eyes told me that she misinterpreted my remark for a moment. When she realized what I was referring to, she said, "If you want to pull out, be my guest, but we're going on."

"Take it easy, Kate. I didn't say anything about pulling out. I just thought that maybe I was entitled to know what's in Mexico that you're so anxious to get to."

She stood up and put her hands on her hips.

"Don't tell me you believe that story about 'Macklin's Treasure'?" she asked.

"I didn't say anything about a treasure, either, but now that you mention it, it's pretty obvious that somebody believes the story."

"You think it's that sheriff in Macklin—I mean, Baxterville?" Sara asked.

"Yes, I do. Do you have someone else in mind?"

Kate threw Sara a quick look, and Sara replied, "No, I don't have anyone in mind."

"How about you?" I asked Kate.

"No," she answered shortly.

"No ideas at all, huh?" I asked them both, and then turned to include Billie.

"Do you intend to go on with us to Mexico?" Kate asked.

"I thought I answered that."

"Then do it, and stop asking questions," she suggested.

"All right," I said, and she and Sara walked over to Billie, so that they didn't hear me finish, ". . . for now."

12

The remainder of our trek through Oklahoma to Texas was relatively uneventful. The amount of conversation that passed between me and Kate was almost nonexistent. Since that night in Anadarko, she seemed to dislike me more than ever, maybe because I was there in her moment of weakness. Or maybe because I was still there, and she was still feeling weak.

Billie continued the art of one- and two-word sentences, so that left me only Sara and Duke to talk to, and since Sara seemed to be inhibited by Kate, I generally talked Duke's ears off, mostly about what a pain in the behind women were.

Once we crossed the Texas border, our trip was about half over. So far nine men had been killed trying to find the treasure, or trying to stop us from reaching Mexico.

Could that be it? I wondered. Maybe the alleged treasure had nothing to do with it. Maybe they were just trying to keep us from getting to Mexico. But why?

At least the possible existence of a treasure gave me a tangible reason to deal with, but if they simply didn't want us to reach Mexico, I had no idea why.

Our first night in Texas I approached Sara with the idea.

"You think someone doesn't want us to get to Texas?" she asked me, frowning.

"It's not that I think so," I told her. "I'm just looking for reasons why we've been attacked twice."

"You don't believe the treasure story?"

"Do you?"

She shrugged. "I don't know. Only Kate would know if it's true or not."

"What about someone not wanting us to reach Mexico. Would you know any reason for that?"

She shrugged again and shook her head. "I honestly can't think of one, Clint."

"Why are you going to Mexico, Sara?"

She stared at me a moment blankly, as if she hadn't heard me, then answered, "Because that's where Kate said we were going."

"You didn't ask why?"

She shook her head.

"You don't wonder why?"

She shook her head again. It seemed to me that she had suddenly withdrawn from the conversation. I didn't want to upset her, so I dropped the matter for the moment.

"Ever been to Texas before?" I asked her, changing the subject.

Her reaction was surprising. She seemed to become alarmed, and snapped, "Why do you ask that?"

"Just making conversation," I told her.

"Sometimes you make too much conversation," she told me. She took my empty plate from me and went back to the fire, where Billie and Kate were.

Now none of them would talk to me.

I walked over to where the horses were tied to make sure Duke was all right.

"How ya doin' boy?" I asked him. He nuzzled my hand while I patted his muscular neck. I was about to return to the wagon when I caught a whiff of something in the air.

It smelled like ham cooking, only we'd eaten bacon and beans. Besides that, the night breeze was blowing the scent of Billie's dinner away from me, not towards me.

Someone else nearby was cooking, and he was camped behind us a ways, depending on how far the scent was carrying. Judging from the strength of the breeze, I didn't figure he was all that far away from us, so I decided to leave Duke where he was.

I walked back to the three women and asked Kate, "Where's that big Colt of yours?"

She looked at me as if she were going to snap my head off, then realized that something was on my mind.

"It's in the wagon," she told me.

"Get it and keep it handy. I'm going for a little walk. Sara, can you handle the Winchester?" I asked, referring to the one they had in the wagon with the Colt.

"Yes."

"Keep it with you. If I'm not back in an hour, I want you to start traveling."

"At night?" Kate asked.

"Yeah, at night. Go about a mile or so down the trail, then pull off again and camp. Keep a lookout, a sharp lookout. Whether you're still here, or down the trail when I come back, I'll whistle like this." I demonstrated, keeping the volume low. "If you hear that you'll know it's me coming into camp. If you hear someone coming, but you don't hear me whistle, shoot first and ask questions later."

"What if you're not back by morning?" Kate asked.

"Then follow the trail to the next town and tell the Sheriff what's been happening. From there, if you're still determined to go on, you'll have to hire someone else."

"Why don't we all just leave now, together?" Sara asked.

I shook my head. "There's someone on our tail," I told her. "I'm going to find out who it is, and maybe who sent them. With a little luck, I'll be back within the hour." Actually, a lot of luck would have helped, but I didn't want to mention that.

"Just do as I say, all right?" I asked the three of them.

They all nodded.

"Good." I stopped at my gear to pick up my rifle, a modified Henry model I was working on. "Wish me luck," I told them. None of them did, but I went anyway.

I was relying on my nose to lead me to them. It hadn't let me down in all the years I'd had it, so I trusted it and trailed along behind it.

Whoever was behind all of these men had sent three the first time, and six the second time. If it hadn't been for Wild Bill and the young Mr. Earp, those six would have finished me for sure. I'd have gotten three or four before they got me, but I would have been dead just the same.

I wondered how many had been sent this time, and were they trailing us, or was it that they just hadn't caught up, yet. They couldn't smell the food from our fire because of the breeze, so it was possible they didn't know just how close they were. I had that advantage and I hoped it would be enough.

When the scent of cooking ham started to get stronger, I started to be a little more careful of where I planted my feet. I had no idea of how good the men I was dealing with were, but I didn't want to chance finding out by stepping on a dead twig or something. In the silence of the night the sound of a dry branch breaking would be like that of a gunshot.

I knew I was real close when I heard someone whistling. Apparently they had no idea of how close together we were camped and were not worried about keeping quiet. I was on the outskirts of somebody's camp.

I had been prepared for a large group of men—six or more—and was surprised to find that the camp was inhabited by only one. He was still whistling while holding a pan over the flame of his camp fire. He looked like a mountain man, dressed in buckskins, with long, unkempt hair and a bushy beard. It appeared I might have been wrong about him following us, but I didn't want to take the chance. I'd have to talk with him before I made up my mind.

I wanted to come in to the camp from behind him, so I began to circle around carefully, until I was directly behind him.

I took my gun from my holster and prepared to start into his camp when suddenly I heard him say, "Took you long enough to git here, whoever you are."

I froze in my tracks, hoping he'd think he'd make a mistake.

"Well, either shoot me in the back or come on in," he said impatiently, "one or t'other."

I decided to take him up on his second invitation, keeping him covered the whole time. I wanted to be ready in case he whirled around with a gun, trying to take me by surprise.

"I'm coming in," I told him.

"I know you are," he said irritably. "I could hear you comin' a mile away. Shoot, all the noise you make when you walk, I couldn't help but hear you comin'."

I stopped right behind him, uncertain about what to do next. He obviously knew I was coming. Did that mean he had a partner somewhere, drawing a bead on me right now? From the looks of the camp—one horse, one set of gear, and only one set of tracks—I gave up that idea quick enough.

"You got yer gun out, I know. Come on around in front of me and set a spell. Keep yer hardware out if it makes you more comfortable, but make some kind of a danged move. I'm gettin' right nervous."

I walked around and stood on the other side of his fire, watching him. He looked up at me, the flame from the fire dancing in his eyes. They were wise eyes, set in a face that might have been young or old, I couldn't rightly tell. It was creased and wrinkled, but it might just have been weatherbeaten rather than old.

"How'd you know I was coming?" I asked him.

"I tole ya, I could hear you. I kin hear a rabbit from a mile off, and you ain't no rabbit, not by a longshot. Set, will ya, I'm gettin' a crick in my neck."

I sat across from him, still with my gun out. He was a big man, but I knew a lot of big men who could move fast when they wanted to, and I didn't plan on getting caught by surprise.

"I could hear ya, all right," he repeated, "and once you got behind me I could smell ya, too."

He was making an effort to sound illiterate, of that I was sure. He was much smarter than he wanted anyone to think, but alternating between "you" and "ya," he was giving himself away.

"Where are you headed?" I asked.

"Oh, that way," he said, just waving his arm negligently.

"From where?"

"That way," he said, waving his arm again.

"What's your name?"

"Bass, what's yers?"

"Adams."

"Pleased to meetcha, Mr. Adams. Where you headed?"

"Mexico."

"Travelin' with company, are you?"

"How'd you know that?"

"Shoot, I kin smell a woman even with the breeze shootin' the other way," he told me. "Fact is, I can smell them on you. More than one have you?"

"I do."

"Wouldn't be up to sparin' one, would you?" he asked, then added, "or maybe just sharin' one?"

In spite of myself I smiled, realizing that his manner was putting me off guard—or would have, if I wasn't aware of it.

"I'm afraid not. They're not really mine."

He nodded, saying, "Just a guide then, that's what you are?"

"That's it."

He nodded, taking his pan from the fire and scraping some of the ham into a not-too-clean-looking tin plate.

"Have some?" he asked.

"No, thanks. I've eaten."

"Gettin' pretty tired of ham," he confided. "Ran out of everything else, includin' coffee." He squinted at me and asked, "You wouldn't happen to have some coffee, would you?"

I nodded. "Back at camp."

"Think we might be able to do a trade, or somethin'?" he asked. "I got some pelts—"

"Maybe some information," I offered.

"What kind of information?" he asked.

"Well, convince me that you're not following me and the women I'm traveling with," I told him.

"Followin' you? What fer?"

"You tell me."

"Cain't, 'cause I ain't." He scooped some ham into his mouth with a makeshift wooden spoon and then asked, "That convince ya?"

"Maybe."

Fact of the matter was, I really didn't think he was on our trail. My decision was made mostly on instinct, but I'd had that just about as long as I'd had my nose, and I had learned to depend on it just as much—maybe more.

"Yeah," I relented, "I'm convinced. We're not far away," I told him, holstering my gun, "and there should be some coffee left."

I helped him break camp and we walked back to where I'd left the women. I was afraid they might have panicked and left, but they were still there. I was so busy talking to Bass that I almost forgot to whistle.

"Hold it a second," I told him, putting a hand on his arm. "I've got to give them the signal."

"You give them women guns?" he asked me.

"I didn't give them to them, but they've got 'em," I told him.

He shook his head.

"Only a dern fool would give a woman a gun," he observed.

I gave them the signal, and then Bass and I walked into camp.

"Ladies, this is Mr. Bass," I told them, "and right now he'd just about give his right arm for some coffee."

They stared at both of us for a few seconds, and then Billie was the first to move, pouring some coffee into a cup and handing it to Bass.

"Much obliged, ma'am," he told her. He took a deep sip and then said, "That's mighty good, little lady," to Billie. She looked at the ground and went back to stand next to Kate.

Kate and Sara were still holding their guns and I told them, "You can put the guns away now, ladies. Mr. Bass is not dogging our trail. In fact, he's not even going in the same direction."

"That's right, ladies," he told them, eyeing the guns in

their hands nervously. "I'm as harmless as a cougar cub."

They didn't look particularly convinced, but Sara took the Colt from Kate and stashed both weapons back in the wagon.

"Billie, would you take Mr. Bass's horse and put him over with ours?" I asked her. She nodded and took the reins from Bass. Kate was eyeing Bass and wrinkling her nose at the mountain man scent of him. Bass was eyeing Kate and Sara, too.

"Mighty fine-lookin' females, Mr. Adams," he told me. "Shame one of them ain't yours."

"Yeah," I told him. "A shame."

Kate took Sara and Billie around to the other side of the wagon and went through the blanket trick. The ladies then retired for the night, while Bass and I had some more coffee and talked.

He told me about some of his experiences, and I related some of mine. We both lied a little and laughed a lot.

"I don't suppose you would have a whiskey around, would you?" he asked.

"Sorry, that's one thing we don't have," I told him.

"Ah well, I thank you for the coffee, anyway."

"You can take some with you in the morning, too," I told him, "along with some beans and bacon. We've got plenty."

"I'm much obliged to you, Clint," he told me. During our story-telling he'd started calling me Clint, while I stuck with calling him Bass.

After an hour or so, I told him a little of what had happened recently, leaving out the fact that the women had been forced into the trip to Mexico by difficult circumstances, but including the fact that someone was on our trail, and that two attempts had been made on us, already.

"Seems to me you been pretty lucky up 'til now," he observed.

"Very lucky," I agreed.

"If I run into anyone headin' your way, I'll surely try and steer 'em in the wrong direction," he promised.

"We'd appreciate that, Bass," I told him.

He finished his coffee and got to his feet, saying, "If you don't mind, Clint, I'll be headin' back to my own camp."

"Why not spend the night here?" I asked.

He smiled and said, "I'd like to, I really would, but that woman smell is a might too strong for me, knowing that I can't touch, and all. You get my meanin'," he explained.

"Sure. I'll get that stuff I promised you." I went to the wagon and wrapped up some beans, bacon and coffee for him.

"I'm really much obliged, Clint," he told me when I handed it to him. "I'm also real glad to have met you and I wish you luck on the rest of your trip."

"Thanks, Bass. Take care of yourself."

"Take care of the little ladies now, ya hear?"

"I will," I promised.

I watched him as he retrieved his horse and headed back to where he'd been camped before. When he was gone I opened my bedroll and tried to go to sleep. I wasn't having much luck anu was wondering why when I sniffed the air and realized what the reason was.

It was like Bass said, the women smell was just too strong.

13

In the morning, Kate's shoulder was colder than ever, and I knew it was because of Bass.

"Some supplies are missing," she snapped as we were packing up to leave.

"Oh?"

"Some bacon, some beans, and some coffee."

"I gave some to Bass."

"You did what? What right do you have giving away supplies that have been bought with my money?" she demanded.

"The man was low on supplies. I just gave him enough to help him a little, out of courtesy."

"Well, next time don't be so damned courteous with my belongings!" she shouted. Sara and Billie were standing off to the side, watching and listening.

"Calm down, Kate," I told her.

"Sure, calm down. We've got killers on our trail, we need all the supplies we've got, you're giving them away, and you want me to stay calm. That's a laugh!"

"Kate—" I began, then looked at Billie and Sara. I took Kate's elbow and drew her away to where the girls wouldn't hear what we were saying.

"Kate, I think we should talk about what happened in Anadarko. We've got to clear the air on this thing."

"I don't want to discuss anything that happened in Anadarko, ever!" she said, her voice insistent, but low enough so that the girls couldn't hear.

"Look, there's no reason for you to feel guilty about what happened, Kate, and we've got to get this cleared up if we're going to keep on traveling together."

"Well maybe I'll just change that."

"How do you mean?"

"I could fire you."

I thought that one over for a moment.

"Yeah, I guess you could. That's certainly your right. Do you think that you and the girls could find your way to Mexico from here?"

"I don't see why not."

"Okay, but do you think the three of you could handle any problems that came up between here and Mexico."

She remained silent, her eyes flashing danger signs. She wanted to tell me that they could, but she knew that wasn't the case.

"Can you handle killers, Kate—because that's what we're up against, here. And I'll tell you another thing."

"What?"

"I've taken this thing kind of personal now. They tried to gun me down in Anadarko, and I don't take something like that lightly."

She stared at me a few moments, head cocked, studying me, then said, "No, I wouldn't think that you would."

"What do you say?" I asked.

She looked at the ground, a move I was used to seeing from Billie, not the bold Kate.

"I still don't want to talk about what happened in Anadarko," she said, then added, "not now. Maybe another time, but not now. I will try to be more . . . civil, for the rest of the trip," she promised. She looked up at me and asked, "Agreed?"

"Agreed."

"Then let's get going."

I helped them finish packing the wagon, and then we moved out. Sara decided she wanted to ride, rather than sit in the wagon, so I saddled one of the extra horses for her, and she rode with me, ahead of the wagon.

"What did you and Kate talk about?" she asked.

"Nothing. We just agreed to try to be more civil with each other for the remainder of the trip."

"I don't believe you," she told me.

I looked at her.

"What's that supposed to mean?" I asked.

"Something happened in Anadarko," she said.

"We told you what happened," I told her.

She shook her head. "Something else."

"Like what?"

"Like what happens between a man and a woman," she said. "Like what happened with us."

"Did Kate tell you that?"

"She doesn't have to," she said loftily. "A woman knows."

I kept quiet and we rode that way for a few more minutes.

"Was it the way it was with us?" she asked, breaking the silence. "Was she as good?"

"Sara—"

"I know. You don't want to talk about it."

"It's not worth discussing," I told her.

"Then you admit it?"

I looked over at her, to see her expression. I expected her to look as if she were jealous, but she seemed amused. She was trying to make me uncomfortable.

I decided to play the same game.

"Actually," I told her, "she was pretty damn good."

"What?" she asked, looking shocked.

"Yeah, she's got one thing you don't, Sara. She's got experience. In a few years, you might even be able to come close to Kate," I predicted.

"Clint Adams," she snapped, "you're a—"

"That makes two of us, sweetheart," I told her.

She stared at me and her face underwent a few changes of expression, until she finally realized what I was doing. Her face relaxed into a wry smile.

"I guess I deserved that, didn't I?" she asked.

"Yes, ma'am," I answered, smiling, agreeing with her, "I guess you did."

14

Soon after we'd crossed into Texas I began to pick up some fresh Indian sign. The last thing I wanted was to attract the attention of the Kiowa or, as we got deeper into Texas, the Comanche.

By 1867, most of the Indian hostility was over and Quanah Parker, the son of a Comanche chief and a captured white girl, and the Kiowa Chiefs, Satank, Satanta and Big Tree, had agreed to settle in the Oklahoma Territory. That arrangement didn't last very long, however, as the white man began to intrude on what was supposed to be Indian land, Quanah Parker and the other Chiefs renewed the hostilities, and Texas was now the main stomping ground of the Kiowa and Comanche.

Catching the Indian's attention would not be very hard, traveling with three women, two of whom had hair that would stand out miles off.

I eased up on Duke until I was riding alongside the wagon, where all three women were riding now.

"Do you ladies have something to put on your heads?" I asked them.

"What do you mean?" Kate asked.

"I mean you and Sara, mainly. Have you got hats or something, anything to cover that hair of yours?"

"What's the matter with our hair?" Sara demanded

from between Kate and Billie.

"It's too damned bright, that's what. Indians have sharp eyes as it is, we don't need to give them any help in spotting us." They had a right to know what we were riding into.

"Indians?" Sara exclaimed.

"That's right. Kiowas. A little later we'll have to start worrying about Comanches. Women with hair any color than black are a curiosity to most Indians. The last thing we need are a band of curious Indians."

"What about Apaches?" Kate asked. She'd obviously heard stories about the Apaches. Truth be told, the Comanches are the reason the Apaches moved on into Mexico. Oh, they cross over now and again, but for the most part Texas was Comanche country, and they were very possessive about it.

"Once we get close to Mexico we can add them to our worries," I told her. "Right now, however, I don't want to run into any of them. We're damn lucky we've come this far without running into the Nez Perces, Utes, Mescalero or any of the others." Now that I had sufficiently frightened them, I went back to the business at hand.

"Hats, kerchiefs, it doesn't make a difference, just cover up your hair if you want to keep it," I told them.

"What about me?" Billie asked.

I looked at her. From far off you might mistake her for a young boy, with her slim figure. The only thing that might give her away was her long hair.

"Dark hair isn't unusual to the Indians, hon, but you might try tucking the length of it into your shirt," I suggested.

Kate began rummaging through the back of the wagon until she came up with a hat and a kerchief. She handed Sara the hat, who piled her hair atop her head and then jammed the hat down over it. A few strands escaped, but not enough to do any damage. Kate tied the kerchief around her head, tucking all of her red tresses underneath it as best she could. I just hoped the Indians wouldn't get close enough to get a good look at their breasts, because there wasn't much we could do about them.

"Now keep a sharp eye out," I told the three of them, and kicked Duke into a canter that took us back to the point.

My eyesight was as good as can be, but even though I hadn't seen hide nor hair of a feathered head, I had the feeling someone was watching. It wasn't unusual for Indians to follow you for miles, playing with your nerves, until they finally decided to move in on you, or let you go. Duke had started to act nervous and I had come to rely on that as a danger sign. That and my instinct about us being watched was enough to really start me to worrying.

I backed Duke up alongside the wagon again and spoke to the women without turning my head.

"Ladies, listen up." I could hear them snap to attention. "We may have company in the next few moments—"

"Indians—" one of them said. I thought it was Billie.

"This is important! We may have company in a few moments, a few hours, or never, but if we do I want you to remember one thing: Indians respect one thing above all else, and that's courage. If we happen to get caught, don't show them that you're afraid. It's all right to be afraid but for God's sake, don't show it. We'll all live longer that way."

None of them answered me, so I said, "Is that clear? Answer me without looking at me."

"Yes," Sara answered.

"Kate?"

"Easy for you to say," she remarked wryly, "but yes, it's clear."

"Billie?"

It took her three tries to get the word out, but she was finally able to whisper, "Yes," just loud enough for me to hear.

"Okay. If we remember that, we'll be fine."

"Hey, Clint," Sara called.

"What?"

"How're your nerves?" she asked, teasingly. I was glad that she could still tease me, under the circumstances, so I decided to give it right back to her.

"Shot," I told her, and rode on ahead.

I hoped that wouldn't actually be the case by the end of the day.

It wasn't.

The remainder of the day passed without incident. Eventually we came to a rock formation that made for a good camp. We were just about enclosed on all sides, and I liked the location so much that we stopped earlier than usual. This drew no comment from the women.

Kate must have really been concerned—or frightened—because under normal circumstances she would have kicked up a fuss about stopping early.

I still hadn't actually spotted any Indians, but that feeling of being watched persisted, even as we set up camp.

"Did you see anything at all today?" Kate asked me as we set out the bedrolls.

"Just sign," I told her. "Mostly Kiowa, some Comanche. I still feel watched, though."

"Is it possible—I mean, could they just . . ."

"Let us go? It's possible. You never know with Indians. They might see us, and just not be interested."

"What do you think the chances of that are?" she asked.

I shrugged.

"That's hard to say," I hedged. "Let's get this fire built."

"Okay."

This was a new Kate. The fire was gone, and the woman it left behind was eager to do as she was told.

I didn't like this one as well.

I scanned the rocks above us. Enclosed as we were, that was the only thing I really had to worry about. I figured to let the women sleep while I kept watch. It sounded gallant of me, but gallant often means the same thing as foolish.

Sara and Kate built the fire while I tended to the horses. While I was unhitching the team from the wagon, I noticed one of them favoring his right foreleg. I'm no smithy, but I knew a stone bruise when I saw one. On top of that, he'd thrown a shoe.

I had a few options. We could leave him behind, or simply tie him to the back of the wagon for the remainder of the trip. Chances were he'd get worse and slow us down if we took him along. Either way we went the other three horses were going to have to pick up the slack, and that might slow us down, too. The other thing was to get him to a smithy, have him reshoed and rested. That would mean finding a small town, because we were a long way from the next major one.

I knew of a town—well, not much of a town, but it had a smithy, a saloon and a hotel, which was all we'd really need. Getting there would mean traveling west for a while, instead of south, but I didn't think Kate would fight me, so that's the way I decided to go.

As I was brushing Duke, Sara came up to me.

"Food'll be ready soon. Billie's starting it now."

"Tell her not to make any bacon or coffee," I told her.

"What about beans?" she asked.

"And jerky, but that'll be it. Chances are they know

exactly where we are, but there's no point in making it easier to find us just in case they don't." If we had any white men on our trail, bacon and coffee odors would carry a long way.

"When did that horse start limping?" I asked, indicating the one who'd thrown a shoe.

"Was he?" she asked. "It must've happened late in the day. I didn't notice."

I hoped it had happened late. If the stone bruise wasn't too bad we might not have to stop for more than a day. Maybe we could even pick up another horse and be on our way.

"We're going to have to detour to take care of him," I told her.

"We'll lose time," she pointed out.

"Maybe not as much as we would if we left him behind and traveled a horse light. We'll go west to a small town I know. We should be able to have him cared for, or pick up another horse."

"I'll tell Kate," she said, starting off.

"I'll tell Kate, Sara. You tell Billie about the food."

She looked at me a moment, then said, "All right, Clint."

Two strong-willed women, Sara and Kate were, but the trip through Indian country seemed to have taken most of the fire right out of both of them. I hoped they'd be O.K. if we ran into trouble.

After caring for Duke I settled down to a meal of beef jerky and beans. Letting them cook the beans was another gallant move. I was responding to them as women, when I should have treated them the same as any other traveler. I was making concessions I shouldn't have been making, and I hoped we wouldn't get burned by them.

I sat next to Kate and told her my plans.

"We'll lose time," she pointed out.

I explained how, by stopping, we might actually end

up saving time. She considered it, then said, "Whatever you think is best, Clint."

"Have you done much traveling, Kate?" I asked her.

"Some, but I've never felt this vulnerable," she told me, rubbing her arms with her hands.

"You wouldn't have wanted me to lie to you about the danger, would you?" I asked.

She looked at me and said, "I might have, but I'm glad you didn't."

We ate in silence for a few moments. She was struggling with a decision, and when she finally made it she broke the silence.

"Clint."

"Yes?"

We were far enough from the two girls for our conversation to be private.

"About what happened in Anadarko," she said.

"Kate—"

"I want to talk about it now," she told me. She sounded sincere, so I let her talk.

"I just want you to know that I don't hold you responsible," she told me. "I came to your room, I caused it to happen, because, at that moment, I wanted it to happen. I'm—I'm even glad it happened."

"So am I, Kate."

"But it mustn't happen again, and it won't. I want you to know that, too. It's nothing personal. I hope you understand."

I didn't, really. Why was she bent on being loyal to a man who was supposed to be dead? I didn't understand, but I told her that I did, because what else could I tell her?

After our meal I saw the three of them huddled together over the fire, talking.

"Ladies, time to turn in. I want to get an early start in the morning."

They all walked over to me and confronted me. Something was on their minds.

"You're going to stay awake, aren't you?" Kate asked, making it sound like an accusation.

"I, uh, just want to keep an eye out," I told them. "Get some sleep—"

"No," Kate told me. "We've decided that Sara will take the first watch, I'll take the second and Billie the third. She'll wake you for the last part of the night."

"I appreciate the offer," I told them, "but—"

"If we were men, would you stay awake the entire night?" Sara asked.

They had me there.

"Well, we appreciate your gallantry, but it has no place here," Kate pointed out, "so you get to sleep and Billie will wake you when it's your watch."

I could see there was no point in arguing with them, and I could see one other thing, too: when it came time for us to deal with the Indians, they'd all be all right. Now all I had to worry about was myself.

15

I slept on the other side of the wagon, as always, with the blanket separating us. I slept damned good, too. I made myself comfortable, with my gun right by my head just in case I needed it right quick.

I put my hands behind my head and listened for the sounds of at least two of the women preparing to go to sleep. I had listened like that every night, but I could never hear much through the double wall of two thick blankets.

I closed my eyes and fell right to sleep.

I didn't know how much time had gone by, but suddenly I was awake and aware that someone was approaching me. It could have been one of the women—who had the watch before mine?—getting ready to wake me for my watch, or it could have been someone else entirely. I played possum, waiting for whoever it was to make his or her move.

Whoever it was walked very lightly, indicating a person who wasn't very big. Soon I could smell the person, and I knew it was a woman, and not a very large one.

It had to be Billie.

I opened my eyes and felt silly when I saw her face. The first thing I noticed were those eyes, big enough to get lost in. The second thing I noticed was that she was barefoot. And naked.

I was startled, but not too startled to stare. Her breasts were small mounds of flesh, smooth and firm, with small, brown nipples that swelled even as I watched. She had an incredibly tiny waist, slim hips and beautifully tapered legs. The patch of hair between her legs was sparse, but what there was on it was black as coal, like the hair on her head. I watched as her tongue flicked out and moistened the full lips of her lovely, rosebud mouth.

What the hell was she doing? We were in the middle of Indian country and she'd chosen this moment to get over her shyness.

"Billie, wha—" I began, but she bent over, breasts swaying ever so slightly, and put her finger to her lips, and then to mine, shaking her head as well. Then she smiled a wide, lascivious smile which I found very odd coming from a face that had previously betrayed nothing but the most benign innocence.

I couldn't believe what was happening, as she spread the length of her body atop mine, a body which was barely more than half the length of my own. She planted her mouth firmly on mine, forcing her tongue between my lips.

"I don't want to die," she whispered into my mouth, and then I understood.

This was her way of preparing herself, in the event that we didn't make it out of Comanche country alive.

I decided to help her . . . and myself, because it wasn't a bad idea.

My hands moved as if they had a life of their own, clamping down on her buttocks, which only just filled my hands. She began to grind her crotch against mine in a circular motion.

Suddenly, she broke the kiss and moved her attention

to my crotch, where she undid my pants, allowing my painful erection to spring free. She caressed it with both hands and I could have sworn I heard her crooning to it. For a fleeting moment I wondered what would happen if Sara or Kate happened to wake up and walk around the wagon, but when Billie allowed my rod to slip between her lips into the depths of her hot, avid mouth, that didn't matter anymore. Nothing mattered but the sensations she was causing.

What had Sara said? Anytime, anywhere . . .

Billie was a small girl—and young, I reminded myself—and I was surprised at how much of me she was able to take into her mouth. She teased me with her tongue and teeth until I was ready to explode, then allowed me to slip free, where the cool night air dried her saliva from me and gave me the chills. I wasn't cold for long, however, because she moved herself up and quickly impaled herself on me.

The heat was intense, and intensely delightful. I watched her face in fascination. Lizzie, the livery girl, Sara and even Kate had enjoyed sex, but this little girl seemed to revel in it. Her eyes were squeezed shut tightly and there was a look of pure rapture on her face and she rode up and down the length of my shaft. I don't think she was even aware of me, but that wasn't enough to keep me from enjoying as well. I began to catch her rhythm and move with her. As she approached orgasm the smile left her face as she clamped her lips tight to keep from shouting. Her tiny fists were beating on my stomach, but I was almost unaware of the blows. All I felt was that great rush building inside of me and I hoped I'd be able to keep quiet when I blew my top.

Her movements became more and more frenzied as she tried to achieve maximum penetration by bringing herself up higher and slamming down on me as hard as she could. Faster and faster she moved, with me trying to keep up, until she was finally ready. When her time came she jammed herself down on me and began to grind herself against me. The cords on her neck stood out, as did mine. We both were preparing to smother the shouts of pure ecstasy that were fighting to get loose. When it was over she stretched out full length on top of me and I could feel her heart beating as fast as mine was.

"Billie—" I began, but she lifted her head and quickly touched my lips with hers. "It's your watch," she whispered. She gave me a fleeting kiss, and then she was gone.

If I hadn't had to reach down to close my pants, it all might have been a dream.

16

At first light I woke them and told them it was time to go. Billie was her old, quiet, shy self, as if nothing had happened between us. I felt good about what had happened with her, because she had needed it. She had needed to get it out of her system, and to feel better about what might happen from here on in. I felt even more sure now that if we crossed paths with Kiowas, or Comanches, she'd react fine.

The town we were headed for was called Comanche Creek, which was odd because, moving to the Southwest as we had to in order to get there, took us away from the heart of Comanche country. You were likely to run into the Pueblo, Hopi, Navaho, or some other less ferocious tribe, rather than the Comanches, but far be it from me to criticize a town for the name it chose.

As I had indicated, it wasn't really much of a town. It was more like an odd collection of buildings that someone had decided to call a town.

We got there by mid-afternoon and by that time the injured horse, tied to the back of the wagon, was limping painfully.

"This is a town?" Sara asked, surveying the wooden and adobe structures which made up Comanche Creek. Hell, there wasn't even a creek nearby.

"It'll have to do," I told her. We rode in and found the Smithy.

"You folks are a ways off the beaten path, ain't ya?" he asked.

He was a big, rawboned man of forty-five or so. He had to be at least six and a half feet tall and, although he wasn't overly muscled, he exuded an aura of raw power.

"Headed for Mexico," I told him, "when one of our horses threw a shoe. You wouldn't happen to have a horse we could buy, would you?"

I got down off of Duke and followed him around to the back of the wagon. The women stayed where they were.

He picked up the horse's leg to inspect the damage.

"Hell, you don't need another horse. I kin fix this'n up good as new."

"Will we be able to pull out tomorrow?" I asked.

"Sure thing, just don't go hitchin' him up to the wagon so fast. Give him another day or so to heal, then he'll be good as new. 'Sides, ain't a horse in town available for you to buy."

"I guess that settles it," I told the women. They all nodded meekly.

"Name's Eustace McClean," the Smithy told me, sticking out a massive hand. Mine got lost in his when we shook.

"Clint Adams. I'm escorting these ladies to Mexico," I said, offering no reason for the trip. I couldn't even be sure of the reason myself although I had some suspicions.

"Ladies," he said. He'd've tipped his hat had he been wearing one.

"Which way is the hotel?" I asked him.

"Down the street a piece, on the right. Saloon on the first floor, rooms on the second."

It was walking distance, so the women got down and

I walked Duke and the wagon inside the livery. While inside McClean pulled me aside.

"Those three are mighty pretty women, friend," he told me, "and this town is full of hardcases. You best be real careful with them, hear?"

"I hear. Thanks for the warning."

That had been the original reason that I hadn't wanted to bring any of them into Anadarko with me, but I couldn't rightly leave them waiting in Comanche country for me this time.

I gave McClean some money and asked him if that would cover the work on the horse, plus housing our gear over night. He gave me some back, then said it was covered. An honest man in the middle of nowhere—which is right where a dishonest man could make a bundle.

We attracted a lot of attention when we entered the saloon, and it sure as hell wasn't because of me. Both Kate's and Sara's shirts were plastered to their bodies by sweat, and they might as well have been wearing nothing. Their breasts stood out prominently and every man in the saloon was taking advantage of that fact to take a good look.

We approached the bar and I asked the pop-eyed bartender if we could get a couple of rooms and some food.

"Sure thing," he said, happily. He took our orders for food and handed me a couple of keys.

"I'll come down for the food," I told him. "The ladies will eat in their room."

You could feel the disappointment in the air, something thick, heavy, and ugly. There were about six men in the room, beside the bartender and, as the Smithy had warned, they were all hardcases.

We took our gear off the bar and went up the stairs to our rooms. There were some whispered remarks behind us, and some laughter, but it all seemed to bother me a lot more than it bothered the women.

"This one will be yours," I told them, giving them the room furthest from the stairs. "To get to yours they'll have to walk past mine."

"Who?" Kate asked, trying to hide a smile.

"Whichever one of those hardcases downstairs works up the nerve first, Kate," I told her. "You three better stay in your rooms until morning. I'll bring your dinner up, and we'll leave before breakfast in the morning."

Sara and Billie walked into the room, but Kate hung back.

"What?" I said.

"You really do take good care of us, don't you?" she asked, her face softening.

"That's what you're paying me for, isn't it?" I asked.

"Probably not nearly enough," she told me.

"We can renegotiate another time," I answered.

"Like hell," she said, and walked into the room, shutting the door behind her.

I went into my room and threw my gear on the bed. I looked out the window at the empty street. Seven men downstairs now knew that there were three women in town. I didn't know what the population of the town was, or how many women there were, but word would soon get around about Kate and Sara. I shook my head, wondering if this had been such a good idea, after all.

When I went downstairs to get the food the number of men in the place had increased. There were five or six more men there, all of whom looked up when they heard me coming down, then looked away when they saw that I wasn't any of the women they had heard about.

The bartender had the food ready on a tray, four dishes of a stew with chunks of meat, potatoes, beans and some bread. It smelled good. I was leery about occupying both of my hands with the tray, but there was no other way, so I picked up the tray and started for the steps.

"Man with three women shouldn't keep them all to hisself," someone said as I approached the steps. I kept silent and went on walking.

"You hear me, stranger?" the same voice asked. "One woman should be enough for any one man. How 'bout sharin' the other two, huh? We'll give 'em back to you in one piece," he added, and the room broke into laughter.

I was ready to drop the tray if anyone made a sudden move, but I made it to the steps without further remarks. They were still working their way up to it.

Upstairs I knocked on the door and Sara opened it to let me in. They had all changed out of their wet clothing, but you still couldn't hide their natural attributes.

"Problem?" Kate asked, seeing the frown on my face.

"I'm starting to think this wasn't such a good idea," I told her, setting the tray down. "I'll eat in here with you."

"Trouble downstairs?" Sara asked.

"Not yet," I said, grabbing a wooden chair, "but it's brewing. Did you bring your guns in?" I asked.

Sara produced the Colt and the rifle.

"When I leave, keep them handy," I told them.

We all set to eating, and agreed that the stew was delicious. That and McClean were probably the only good thing about Comanche Creek.

When we were done I gathered the plates and piled them on the tray.

"I'll bring these downstairs," I told them, also intending to get myself a bottle of whisky. "After that I'll go to my room. Keep those guns handy, and call me if you need me. I'll hear you."

"You worry a lot," Kate told me, but I could see she appreciated it.

"Lock the door when I leave," I told them. I waited in the hall until I heard the lock, then proceeded downstairs with the tray.

"That was delicious," I told the bartender.

"I'll tell my wife," he said, grinning happily. He was a portly man of about fifty who looked out of place among the hardcases. I gave him some money and asked for a bottle.

"You and those women gonna have a party upstairs, stranger?" the same voice asked from behind me—close behind me. The owner of the voice had walked up to me until he was right behind me.

I looked over my shoulder at him. He was as tall as me, but leaner, and older. He needed a shave and a bath, and a miracle for his breath.

"I don't like somebody breathing down my neck, friend," I told him, picking up the bottle from the bar. I turned and moved into him and he almost tripped getting out of the way. That set the room to laughing again, but he didn't like it this time because they were laughing at him.

"You gonna share those women?" he asked belligerently.

I turned back to him and said, "That's up to the women, friend."

He smiled, revealing a gap where his front teeth used to be. Probably didn't move out of someone's way fast enough, but he hadn't appeared to have learned from it.

"Then I guess I—uh, we'll just go on up and ask them ourselves," he told me, scanning the room for volunteers.

"I guess you better," I told him. I walked to the stairs, mounted two of three of them, and then turned back to face the room. I was high enough for all of them to see me.

"Just one more thing," I said to the spokesman.

"What's that?"

"I'll shoot the first man I see near the door of those ladies' room," I told him, and the room at large, then turned and continued up the stairs.

17

It was long after dark when there was a timid knock at my door. I opened it up without asking who it was, but with my gun in my hand.

"Hey, I don't think you're gonna need that gun, Mister," the girl in the hall said. She was a pretty little thing wearing an off-the-shoulder blouse that showed her small but ripe breasts off to their best advantage.

"Hello," I said. "Who are you?"

"My name is Emelita. Can I come in, please?"

I stepped back and allowed her to enter. I shut the door and put up my gun. She began to stroll around the room, hands clasped behind her back.

"What can I do for you, Emelita?" I asked.

She turned to face me, pushing her little breasts out with a deep breath.

"My daddy runs this dump," she told me. "I heard that there was a stranger in town and I wanted to see what you looked like."

She looked me up and down. I had my shirt off and was barechested, but kept my pants on. I hadn't gotten around to yanking off my boots, yet.

"I like what I see," she told me.

"Well, so do I," I answered. She was a tease. I wondered how she survived in this town.

Or was she just a tease?

What she did next answered that question pretty quick.

She eased that off-the-shoulder blouse off completely, and stood there with her proud little breasts totally naked. Her nipples, dark brown with wide aureoles, were starting to get hard and her breathing began to quicken.

"The men in this town are pigs," she told me, cupping her breasts in her hands, tweaking nipples into life. "You're a real man, stranger, I can tell."

She eased her skirt off and was wearing nothing underneath. For such a little girl she had a startling amount of pubic hair which I found strangely appealing.

Something about this was all wrong, though. As she came closer, as I felt the heat of her body, I realized that this was not a spur of the moment thing. She knew exactly what she was doing, as if someone had told her just what to do.

Like get my attention, and keep it.

I grabbed my gun, ran out of my room and down the hall to Kate's and the girls.

I banged on the door, tried the knob, found it locked. I banged on the door again.

"Kate! Sara!"

Something was wrong. They were in there but they weren't alone. I cursed myself for giving myself away to whoever was in there with them.

I couldn't go busting in now without getting myself shot. There was only one way now.

There was a window at the end of the hall, and theirs was the last room. I started for the window, then turned and found Emelita, fully dressed, standing in the hall.

"You knock on that door to warn them," I told her, "and you won't live to see the outcome."

She believed me, and ran downstairs, which was probably just as bad. Now the men downstairs would know something was wrong.

I opened the window and got out on the ledge, which was wide enough for me to negotiate comfortably. I eased myself over to the window and peered inside.

There were four of them in the room with the three of them. There was one man holding each woman while a fourth had obviously started undressing all three. He had them all topless and was in the act of fondling Sara's breasts when I went through the window.

The fourth man turned away from Sara in time for my bullet to catch him square in the belly, where I was pretty sure it wouldn't go right through him. The other three men let the women go and alertly the three girls hit the floor. The three men went for their guns, but mine was out already. They might have been hardcases, but they weren't gunhands. When the shooting stopped they all had one thing in common. They were dead.

At that moment the door was kicked in and three or four more men burst into the room, guns drawn.

I turned to face them, knowing full well that I only had two bullets left in my gun. Suddenly there was a shot from my right and one of the men fell. I squeezed off my next to last bullet and another went down. The men behind them tried to escape their falling bodies, but got tangled up. I was about to fire my last round when a much louder shot sounded from the hallway, a shotgun blast.

"Get out of here, the lot of yer!" a voice bellowed from outside the room, "before I tear inta all of ya with this here scattergun. Move I tell ya!"

They moved, as if the voice were the voice of God.

I looked over at Sara, who was lying on her belly with the big Colt in her hand, ready to fire again if need be.

Someone stepped into the room and I swung back to the door, gun ready, but the danger was passed. The man in the room with us was Eustace McClean, holding a shotgun in his massive hands.

"Are you all O.K.?" he asked.

The women grabbed for their shirts and began putting them on. McClean watched with a smile on his face, but his look was one of appreciation, not lust.

"I guess we're all okay," I told him. "Thanks to you."

He surveyed the room, which was also filled with six dead men.

"Seems to me you done all right on yer own," he remarked. "You kill all these?" he asked.

"All but that one," I told him, pointing to the one Sara had shot. I pointed to Sara, who was still holding the Colt, and added, "She got him."

But he was looking at me, wondering how I'd been able to gun down five men without catching a bullet myself.

"I guess you people should be all right now. I'll take my leave and see you in the morning. I don't think anyone'll be bothering ya the rest of the night."

I hoped not.

"Thanks for your help," I told him.

He was shaking his massive head wonderingly.

"Between you and these ladies here, I ain't so sure you needed it, but yer welcome all the same. Good night, ladies."

He left, closing the door behind him. It remained ajar, broken from having been kicked in.

"Are they just going to leave these men lying here?" Kate asked, surprised.

"I guess someone will be along in the morning to clean up," I told her. "But I suppose you three had better come along to my room. You've got no window and your door doesn't lock."

I received no argument from any of them. At that moment, I wondered if each of them had any idea what had gone on, at one time or another, between all four of us. Had they exchanged notes?

I wondered.

The rest of the night passed without further incident. Kate and Billie had shared the bed in my room, while Sara and I slept on either side of it. I woke first and roused the three of them, and we walked on over to the livery.

"'Morning," Eustace McClean greeted us.

"Good morning. How's he doing?" I asked, indicating the horse that was responsible for this whole side trip.

"He's fine. I took care of that bruise and gave him a new shoe. Like I said, don't be quick to hitch him up and he'll be good as new."

"About last night," I brought up. "Is there any law in this town I should talk to?"

"Oh, 'scuse me for not tellin' you," he said. He removed his leather apron and showed me the star pinned to his chest.

"I'm the only law here, and I took care of everythin' for you. There's nothing more for you to do 'cept leave town."

"The sooner the better," I told him. "There was a girl last night—" I began, but he cut me off.

"Emelita. I know, her daddy runs the saloon and tends bar himself. One of them fellers you shot was her man. Her pa's right happy you kilt him. Seems he was a bad influence on his little girl."

"I can believe that," I told him. He helped me hitch the team up, and when I saddled up old Duke we were ready to leave.

"You might be able to use this, too," he said, dropping a large bundle into the wagon.

"What's that?" I asked.

"Some supplies. You still got a ways to go on your trip. Good luck to you all."

The three women each said, "Thank you," and waved to big Eustace McClean.

Once out of town Kate, holding the reins in her hands, said, "Well, back to Indian country."

"We'll travel Southeast on a diagonal track," I told her. "We might be able to avoid the Kiowa that way."

"And the Comanches?" Sara asked.

"Once we get back on our trail, we may still have to deal with them," I explained.

They looked at each other, then back at me, and I just shrugged and said, "Cover up your hair, ladies, and let's get moving."

18

To my surprise, and to the delight of Kate, Sara, and Billie, we eventually crossed the border into Mexico without attracting attention from the Kiowa or Comanches. I was still convinced they were on our trail, but for some reason they chose not to make a move.

Once we were in Mexico, we stopped and looked back at Texas.

"We made it," Kate breathed.

"We made it this far," I told her. "I assume we've still got a little ways to go yet before we get where you really want to go."

She looked at me.

"You deserve to know, Clint, and I wish I could tell you, but you will know in due time. I promise."

"Sure."

"You know what?" Sara asked.

"What?" I asked.

"I think I'm a little disappointed."

"Why?"

"I think I was actually looking forward to seeing a Comanche up close."

I had chosen that moment to look up at a rise of ground ahead of us.

"Would you settle for an Apache?" I asked.

They all looked up and saw him, one lone brave, sitting straight up on his pony, watching us. From what I could see, he was armed with only a bow. He seemed content just to watch us; we were in for the same kind of trip we took through Texas, traveling with shadows. I hoped.

The Comanches had chosen to let us go for some reason, but we might not be that lucky with the Apaches.

"What do we do now?" Kate asked.

"We keep going . . . and wait." I looked at Kate and asked, "Where are we going, Kate?"

"South."

"To where?"

"Just South. When we get there, then you'll know."

I didn't like traveling blind, but I'd come this far, had taken half her money, and had killed a lot of men. I figured I might as well go all the way.

As we started up, the brave wheeled his pony around and disappeared over the rise. By the time we had crested the rise and started down the other side, the brave was gone. The only sign that he'd been there were the tracks of his unshod pony.

"Where'd he go?" Sara asked, looking around.

"He's around," I told her.

I gave Duke a little kick and we scooted on ahead of the wagon. I didn't really believe that our luck could hold out for the whole trip. The itch in my back was different from the one I had in Texas.

I would have bet the whole four hundred I was getting for this trip that the Apaches wouldn't be as understanding about Mexico as the Comanches and Kiowas were about Texas.

I would have won.

They waited until the next day, however. We camped and I knew they were out there, watching. I even told Billie to go ahead and make the bacon and coffee. I was thinking, if this is going to be our last meal, we might as well enjoy it. If it was going to be my last night on earth, I would have liked to have a woman too, but which one? I decided not to dwell on that for too long. If each of them had no idea that I had been friendly with the others, to bring up the subject might deprive me of one last night.

I think I preferred the Apaches.

They didn't wait long once we'd broken camp. We were traveling about an hour when one of the women screamed. I turned and saw an Apache arrow imbedded in the wagon.

"That's it," I told them. "Get those horses moving!"

They seemed to come from nowhere, five from one side, five from the other. Ten, a small party. We got lucky.

Maybe.

Kate whipped the team into action and I followed with Duke. A few arrows flew through the air, but I figured they'd be content just to run us into the ground. They'd do it, too. We were going to have to find someplace to make a stand.

I kept my eyes open and then I saw it. Rocks and trees had joined together to form a semicircular wall. If we set the wagon right across the front of it, we'd have a small hole to crawl into.

I urged Duke on and caught up with the wagon. I called Kate's name and pointed where I wanted her to go. She got the idea. Once she'd pulled in front of our hole, I yelled for them to get behind the wagon. I put Duke behind the wagon, too, then cut the team loose from it. I didn't want the horses getting spooked and taking the wagon with them. I left the second team tied behind it, though. If by some miracle we outlasted the Apaches, we'd need them.

I cut the team free and dove behind the wagon just as

the first hail of arrows hit. Sara had the Colt, Kate the rifle. I grabbed my Winchester and gave it to Billie. Four against ten, and I wasn't all that sure any of the three of them could hit anything more than four feet away. At the very least though, they'd make a lot of noise, which would make the Apaches think twice about rushing us.

"Don't waste any of your shots," I told them, just in case they could hit what they aimed at.

The Apaches made one rush. I got one, one of the women got the other, and then they backed off.

It stayed quiet for a while.

"What are they doing?" Kate asked.

"They're waiting."

"For what?"

I shrugged. "Who knows? They're good at waiting. They want us to get nervous and maybe make a run for it. If they can catch us out in the open . . ." I let it trail off.

"What would they do to us?" Sara asked.

I put my back against a rock and began to reload.

"They'll probably kill me," I told them.

"And us?" Billie wanted to know.

I looked at all three of them waiting for an answer, their eyes fixed on mine hopefully.

"They'll keep you alive a while," I told them, deciding not to lie to them. They wouldn't have believed a lie anyway, not at this point.

"When do you think they'll come at us again?" Kate asked.

"When they feel like it. Billie, you watch for a while. Sara, did you bring the supplies in from the wagon?"

"Right here," she said, picking up the bag McClean had given us.

"Break out some jerky. We might be here for a long time."

I ate some of the beef strips, but the three of them had

no appetite. Kate crawled over by Billie, to help her watch, and Sara moved over by me.

"Did you reload?" I asked her.

"Yes. Clint?"

"What?"

"I wish we could be together again, before we die," she told me. I looked at her and tried a smile out on her.

"So do I, kid."

"Here they come again!" Kate called.

"Wait for a good shot," I told them.

They came all at once, screaming and showering us with another hail of arrows. I got one more of them, but none of the women hit any. Still, they drew back to make us wait again.

"Everybody all right?" I asked.

We all were, but how long that would last I didn't know. We'd gotten three of them, which cut the odds down a little, but who knew whether or not there were more on the way? I was hoping that maybe a Mexican border patrol might hear the shooting and come to investigate, but that was a long shot.

I sat back down again, to reload.

"I haven't got much ammunition left," Sara told me.

"You can use mine," I told her. It would fit her Colt, too, but the ammunition would go that much faster. I was also going to have to split my rifle ammo with Billie. At that rate, it wouldn't last long at all.

"There's one coming," Billie called out. We all got up and looked over the wagon.

"Only one?" Sara asked.

Sure enough, one brave was approaching on foot, carrying a lance.

"What does he want?" Kate asked.

"I think he wants to talk," I told her. I holstered my gun and stood up.

"You're going out there?" Kate asked.

"Remember what I told you about the Indians respecting courage? I'll be all right. Let's hear what they have to say."

I stepped around the wagon, waiting for a couple of dozen arrows to rip me apart. I approached the brave, who had come as far as he was going to come and was now waiting for me to reach him.

"You speak English?" I asked him.

He looked at me blankly, then said, "I speak white man's tongue."

"Good," was all I could think to say.

"We want women with bright hair," he told me, "and big chest." He patted his chest for emphasis. "You keep small one," he added, generously.

"We have supplies," I told them, "and horses. You can take them." I was talking about the extra team. Before I'd give them Duke, I just might have let them have the women with the bright hair.

He shook his head.

"We want women. You fight for them. You win, you go. You lose, we take all women, kill you, maybe kill skinny one. You fight," he said, banging his chest, "one brave."

It sounded like the best chance we had. He wasn't all that much bigger than I was. If I fought him and won, they'd let us go. If he gave his word, I knew that was what they would do. Indians weren't like white men. Their word meant something.

"You think. We talk later," he told me, and turned around to go back from where he came. I walked back to the wagon, glancing behind me from time to time.

"What do they want?" Kate asked anxiously.

"You," I told her.

"What? Me?"

"Well not just you. They want the women with the

bright hair and the big chest."

She and Sara stared at me, then Kate said, "If this wasn't so ludicrous, it would be funny."

"W-what about me?" Billie asked.

"They said I could keep you," I told her.

She became embarrassed, probably thinking about that night we had together, and turned her head away.

"What did you tell them?" Sara asked.

"I offered them the horses and supplies."

"And?"

I looked at her. "After all, Kate, they are men," I told her. What man in his right mind would take horses and food over two beautiful, full-bodied, bright-haired women?

"You—" she started to get angry.

"You don't think I agreed, do you?"

"Well, what then?" she demanded.

"They gave me an alternative."

"What alternative?"

"A contest, a fight between me and one brave. If I win, we go free, if they win . . . I die, and they get the three of you."

"That sounds fair," Sara admitted. We all looked at her and she said, "Well, I mean, it's fairer than anything —I mean, uh—I'm sorry."

"Don't be sorry," I told her. "It's our only chance. Besides, he didn't look too tough."

"Uh-oh," Billie said, suddenly.

"What's wrong?"

She pointed out towards where my opponent was waiting for my answer. I stood up and looked out with her. What I saw was an Apache who was at least six feet eight inches tall, and almost as wide. If I didn't know any better, I would have said that the remaining seven braves had joined together and become one big one.

"That's not the same brave," I told them. Sara and Kate looked out also.

"I guess the other one was just the spokesman," Kate offered. "That one is the one you have to fight."

He was standing with his feet apart; his legs were like tree trunks, his great arms folded across his chest.

"Maybe there's another way," I said, hopefully.

We all thought for a moment, then looked at each other.

"There's no other way," I said, for all of us.

"If you win—" Kate began.

"If he wins," Sara said, so low I could barely hear her. "Do you see the size of that Apache?"

"If you win," Kate persisted—bless her heart—"will they really let us go?"

"I've never known an Apache to break his word."

"How many Apaches have you known?" Sara asked.

I frowned at her.

"Good luck, Clint."

It didn't matter who said it, because it came from the three of them.

"To all of us," I added. I took off my gunbelt and gave it to Kate, then walked around the wagon to have the biggest fight of my life.

I approached the brave and asked him, "What weapons?"

He smiled and growled, "Not need weapons." He opened both hands wide and held them up for me to see. They were massive, thick-fingered, callused. "These weapons," he told me, and lunged for me.

If I had an advantage it was that I moved faster than he could. I ducked under his lunge and drove a right into his belly. It was like hitting a slab of rock. I swung my leg around behind him, trying to knock him off balance, but his tree-trunk legs were planted firmly and my leg just bounced off his. He swung his right in a backhand and caught me on the shoulder. It felt like I was hit by a horse and I went sprawling.

He was faster than I had first thought, and that advantage I had mentioned shrank to almost nothing.

I scrambled to my feet just in time to avoid being stomped by a giant moccasin.

I turned to face him, and he was smiling, advancing on me slowly. Behind him I could see the wagon, with the three female heads peering over the top.

Most of my fighting had been done with guns. I could do almost anything with a gun. I wasn't as confident with my hands. That was why, back in Baxterville, just before all of this began, when Shagan had come at me in the saloon, I had picked up a chair and flattened him with it. When I get into a fight, I pick up the first thing handy. The only problem here was, we were fighting in an open clearing where there wasn't anything for me to pick up, except sand and stones that were too small to do any damage.

I backed away as he came towards me, then when he charged me again I bent over, hoping to upend him over my back. He was too big and too heavy. He grabbed me around the waist and picked me up, upside down. If it hadn't been so serious, I would have felt embarrassed to be picked up that way in front of the women. Or at the way he dropped me on my head, then kicked me in the ribs. I tried to roll with the kick, then kept on rolling away from him. When I got far enough away I struggled to my feet, but the pain in my side kept me from standing up straight. I grabbed at it, hoping my ribs weren't broken.

He was walking up to me, a big, confident smile on his broad, Apache face. I'd been backing away from him for so long I did the last thing he expected: I charged at him as fast and as hard as I could, and butted him in the face with my head. We both went flying, me with stars floating before my eyes. He staggered back and almost fell, which was a moral victory for me. From the ground I watched him as he dropped his hands from his face and smiled at me through the blood that covered it. There was so much I didn't know if it was coming from his nose or his mouth. He didn't seem to care. He was smiling and walking towards me again. The man had no respect for me at all.

Now I *was* embarrassed.

My head was buzzing from the butt and I just lay there while he came closer and closer. When he was within striking distance I lashed out with my right foot as hard as I could and caught him just below the knee of his right leg. I followed that by doing the same thing to his other leg. He bent over to grab his shins and, bracing myself against the ground, I lashed out and kicked him full in the face.

He still didn't fall. He backed up a lot and stood there shaking his head, showering me with drops of blood. Now I knew his nose was broken, because it was smashed flat against his face. I didn't know what was holding him up, but if I was going to finish him now was the time. I charged him, and he stood his ground, waiting for me. I charged right into his open arms, and then they closed around me, and I knew I'd had it.

He increased the pressure in his massive arms and I could feel my spine cracking. He was breathing hard in my face and his breath was fetid, but that was the least of my problems. Already I could feel myself going under, and by the time he cracked my back and killed me, I probably would be unconscious and unaware that I was dying.

I heard a funny kind of sound, a croaking or humming, and I realized it was him, laughing in my ear while he squeezed the life out of me.

When the blackness came, I almost welcomed it.

19

The sun was a big, yellow, hot ball and it was about an inch from my nose. I blinked my eyes a few times and it retreated up into the sky where it belonged. The first thing I realized was that I wasn't dead.

The second thing was that my back was killing me, but that was all right, because that's how I knew I wasn't dead.

My head was in somebody's lap, and when I looked up to see who it was I saw Sara, looking down at me with concern written all over her face. Almost made getting a cracked back worth it.

"D-did we win?" I managed to croak out.

She smiled and said, "No, Clint, you lost."

I frowned. That didn't make sense. If I lost, why was I alive, why was Sara still here, and why was she smiling?

"But we got saved," she added.

"Saved? By who?"

She nodded her head and I looked in that direction. There were about twelve cowpokes milling around the wagon, some mounted, some on foot. Billie was doing something in the back of the wagon, and Kate was talking to one of the men on foot.

"Who are they?" I asked, sitting up.

"Right now they're the men who saved your life—all of our lives," she told me, stroking the back of my hair with her hand.

"Yeah, but who—" I started to ask again, then it dawned on me.

"You know them, don't you?" I asked her.

She didn't answer, just kept staring straight ahead.

"I mean, wherever they came from, that's where we were going, isn't it?" I asked further.

She tossed her hair and got to her feet.

"You'll have to ask Kate, Clint," she told me. I got to my feet, my back protesting every move, and she reached over to help me. "I'm glad you're all right, Clint. You were wonderful out there."

"Yeah, I was great. I'm glad we're all okay."

We walked to the wagon and Sara started helping Billie. I walked around the wagon to get to Duke, and my guns. As I bent over to retrieve my gunbelt I heard the distinctly familiar sound of the hammer being cocked on a revolver. I turned my head and saw Kate and the man she had been talking to. He was holding the cocked gun, and it was pointed right at me.

"I can't let you pick that up, Mister," he said to me. He was blonde, in his late twenties and the hand holding the gun was very steady. He knew how to use it.

"Just ease off that trigger, son," I told him. I backed away and showed him my hands.

"Kate, what's going on?" I asked.

"I'm sorry, Clint. You'll just have to do what he says for a while. It'll all be explained to you soon enough."

"Sure."

Sara and Billie walked around the wagon to stand next to Kate and the man with the gun.

"He'd better not be hurt, Lam," Sara warned him.

The man looked at Sara, and then back at me with a puzzled look on his face. I didn't like the implication.

"If he does what he's tole," he told her, "he won't get hurt, Sara."

"See that he doesn't."

The three women went around to get into the wagon. The man with the gun approached me, mumbling, "See that he doesn't get hurt," to himself. He prodded me with the barrel of the gun—hard enough to hurt—and said, "Get up on your horse, friend."

I got up on Duke and Blondie—Lam, Sara had called him—forgot about mumbling and passed his eyes appreciatively over Duke.

"Nice horse."

"Thanks. Listen, you're not going to leave my guns behind, are you?"

He looked exasperated and turned to Kate.

"He don't want his guns left behind," he complained.

Sara jumped down and said, "I'll get them." She gathered them up, put them in back of the wagon, then climbed up again.

Lam looked up at me and asked, "Happy?"

"Thanks."

He pulled his bandanna from around his neck and offered it up to me.

"What's that for?"

"Your eyes."

"What?"

"You got to be blindfolded, now c'mon," he snapped impatiently.

"Clint?" Sara called.

I wheeled Duke around and Lam had to duck to keep from being knocked over by his massive neck. "Yeah?"

She held out her kerchief and I reached over and took it.

"Thanks."

I tied it around my eyes, then felt Duke's lead being

taken. I couldn't do anything but sit and wait.

You don't know how long a long time is until you've been made to spend it blindfolded. I had no idea in what direction we were headed. I knew when we were traveling across the flats, and I knew when we were climbing, whether it be a small rise, a hill, or a mountain, but I was totally lost when it came to direction.

At one point, feeling the wagon close at hand, I yelled out, "Hey, Kate."

"What?" her voice came back.

"Do I still get paid for this part of the trip?"

"You'll get paid, don't worry."

Then a male voice, probably Lam, said, "Yeah, you'll get paid, all right." A couple of men laughed, and then we went back to traveling in silence.

When they stopped and finally removed the blindfold, the sun had already gone down a ways. I looked around and saw that we were setting up camp.

"Are we here?" I asked.

"We're here," Sara told me, jumping down from the wagon, "but we're not quite there yet."

"Can I get down?"

"Less'n you wanna spend the night in the saddle," Lam threw in.

"No," I remarked, climbing down from Duke's back painfully, "the whole day there was enough."

There was a flurry of activity as the horses were cared for and the fire was built. I insisted on caring for Duke myself and thanks to Kate, I was allowed to do so.

I joined her by the fire later, for a dinner of bacon, beans, potatoes, and bread. The coffee was hot and tasted good after a long day in the saddle.

"Tell me, am I a prisoner, or what?"

She thought it over a moment, then answered, "More like a guest, but one who gets a lot of attention."

"Meaning I'll be watched—and blindfolded—until we get where we're going."

"It won't be long. We'll be there tomorrow," she assured me. I opened my mouth to ask a question, but she said hurriedly, "Don't ask me anymore questions, Clint, please."

"Okay, all right. No questions."

We finished the rest of the meal in silence. Across the camp I saw the blonde, Lam, talking to Sara. Their discussion quickly took on the appearance of an argument. Sara turned to walk away, but he grabbed her arm and pulled her back. I started to get up, but Kate said, "Don't. Let them be. She can handle him."

I continued to watch and Kate proved right. Sara shook off his hand and said something that snapped his head back, as if she'd struck him. Then she walked off.

I finished my food and dropped the tin plate for somebody else to clean. I went over to check Duke and found Sara there, feeding him some sugar.

"That stuff's no good for him," I told her.

"Oh, pooh. Who cares, he loves it. Here, big boy, have some more." She gave him the last of it and he gobbled it up.

"He's so beautiful," she said, patting his neck.

"You're going to spoil him on me," I told her. "Or do you figure that I won't have too much need of him soon?"

She turned to face me.

"Don't be silly. Nothing's going to happen to you."

"Does your friend Lam know that?"

"What Lam knows doesn't mean anything, it's what he's told," she explained.

"Is he the number one boy?" I asked.

She opened her mouth to answer, then thought better of it and shut it again.

"I know, I know, don't ask any more questions."

"Look, Clint, trust me. Nothing's going to happen to you. I'm going to see to that."

"Trust you, trust Kate, trust everybody. Am I going to get my money?"

She smiled. "You're going to get more money than you ever dreamed of," she promised.

"Is that so?"

At that point Kate came over and said, "Sara, help Billie clean up."

"Okay." She touched my hand and said, "See you later."

We both watched Sara walk to the fire to help Billie with the clean up chores.

"She's got it bad for you, Clint," Kate told me.

"You think so?"

"I know so."

"She says I'm going to get paid and sent on my way, that nothing's going to happen to me. What do you say?"

"It's not up to me," she answered without looking at me. She put her hand on Duke's nose and started stroking it.

"Who's it up to?"

She dropped her hand and said, "Look, Clint, I'll promise you this much. I'll do what I can to see that you get everything that's coming to you. I appreciate what you did for us, I really do. I'll—I'll do what I can," she said again and abruptly turned and walked away.

I brushed Duke down and turned to find Lam approaching me.

"Time to turn in, partner."

"You going to show me to my bed?" I asked.

He smiled at me and put a heavy hand on my shoulder.

"I'm gonna tuck you in, friend."

"I can't wait."

He walked me to a place they had set out for me, away from everyone else.

"Put your hands behind you," Lam told me.

"You're not going to tie my hands, are you?" I asked stupidly.

"Yes, I am."

"Where am I going to go? I don't even know where we are. How am I going to sleep?"

"After the trip we had today, not to mention what you went through this morning, I don't think a little rope could stop you."

Tying my hands he said, "I saw what you did to that big Indian. Messed up his face pretty good."

"Didn't do much good, though, did it? If you hadn't come when you did I'd be dead."

"That's true," he admitted graciously. "I guess I kinda saved your life, didn't I?"

I tried to get my hands comfortable as I said, "Yeah, I guess you did. What happened, anyway?"

He shrugged, turning me around to face him.

"We heard the shots and came a-running. Them Apaches jest turned tail and ran. You know, you don't have to feel so bad about not taking that big Indian."

"Why's that?"

"Hell, I put two slugs in him and he still jumped on his horse and high tailed it away from there."

He was shaking his head in admiration—for the Indian, I think, certainly not of me.

"Well," I said, "I guess I should thank you for saving my life."

"Yeah, I guess you should," he agreed, but then he poked me in the chest with his finger for emphasis as he added, "but don't think that makes us friends, or nothin'."

"Probably nothing," I remarked.
"What?"
I shook my head. "Nothing."

20

I had barely opened my eyes the next morning when they slapped the blindfold back on and practically tossed me up onto Duke.

"What's the rush?" I asked.

Lam's voice answered. "Apaches. We don't want that party to go for reinforcements and catch up to us. Besides, we want to get where we're going before dusk."

I sat on Duke, waiting to get started, when the wagon pulled up alongside me.

" 'Morning ladies," I called out.

Sara and Kate replied, but I didn't hear Billie. Still shy.

We traveled at a brisk pace most of the morning. I could tell when we were approaching midday because the top of my head was starting to get warm, and I could just see the sun above the blindfold. I couldn't see out, but I could see up.

And I could hear.

I heard when Lam shouted, "Oh, shit!" and when Kate yelled, "Oh, no!"

"Let's move it!" Lam shouted.

I heard their horses break into a run, and Kate shouting at her team. Wherever they were running to, they were going to run without me. Hands tied, blindfolded,

I'd never be able to keep up with them—and I had a fair idea what they were running from.

Suddenly I heard Sara's voice.

"Wait!" she shouted. I heard a sound, as if she'd jumped off the wagon, then the sound of her running toward me.

"Sara, come back!" Kate yelled. There was a short pause, then I heard Kate shout at the team again, and off they went.

"Clint, bend down!" I heard Sara shout. I leaned to my right and the blindfold was pulled from my eyes. I was quick enough to keep my eyes shut, and then open them into slits. She untied my hands, and then she yelled, "Look!"

I turned and opened my eyes. Through the brightness I saw them. Thirty, maybe forty Apaches, bearing down on us. The rest of our party was way ahead of us, and we were between both groups.

"Let's go," I told her, reaching down. I grabbed her arm and she grabbed mine and I lifted her up behind me.

"Go, Duke, go!" I told the big fella. He broke into a run and gradually began to increase his speed. I could feel his massive muscles bunching beneath my legs. Duke was the biggest, fastest animal I had ever ridden, or seen, for that matter. We took off after the rest of our party, and then I got an idea. Instead of riding in the same direction, I veered off and began to ride towards the mountains on our right.

"Where are we going?" Sara shouted.

"Away," I told her.

I was hoping the Apaches would let us go and follow the rest. I looked behind us when we changed direction. My plan had partly worked. Four Apaches veered off and followed us, the rest took off after Kate, Lam, and the rest.

"Here," Sara said, handing me something from behind.

It was my gun.

She had the belt slung over her shoulder, and my rifle in her other hand. I hadn't noticed before.

With the gun in my hand, I thought about turning and fighting, but then I had Duke beneath me. He could outrun any horse in the world, and he could run all day.

"Okay, Duke," I told him, "we're going to run their legs off."

They were singleminded in their pursuit of us, and their effort was admirable, but little by little the distance between us began to increase, until we could no longer see them, only the dust they were kicking up.

And then not even that.

Still, I kept Duke going and going, until I thought he couldn't keep it up—and yet he did.

We reached the mountains and I stopped him.

"Are we stopping?" Sara asked. Her arms were around my middle, holding tightly. I could feel her shaking.

"Just long enough to let Duke catch his breath," I told her.

"Then what?"

"Then we'll go up some more. We should find a place to camp. I want to talk to you."

She fell silent, and I asked Duke to climb, knowing he was beat, but knowing he'd do it.

"We won't go far, big boy," I told him, patting his neck. "Then we'll rest."

Up we went. I kept the pace slow, for Duke's sake, while keeping an eye out behind us. At the first sight of an Apache Duke's brief respite would be over. Luckily, the Apaches seemed to have given up on us.

We reached a fair-sized shelf of rock that I figured would make a good enough campsite.

"We'll stop here," I told her. It was approaching dusk and I didn't want to travel in the mountains in the dark. Duke was as surefooted as a mountain cat, but I didn't want to take any chances.

We had my bedroll and a blanket, but no supplies. We'd have to do without eating and without coffee. Food I could do without, but it got cold in the mountains at night. Coffee would have helped. We'd just have to rely on the blanket, bedroll, and each other.

I unsaddled Duke and rubbed him down.

"You did good, big boy," I told him, affectionately. "I'm sorry I don't have a reward for you."

"I do," Sara said. She came forward with some sugar in her hand and he snatched it from her hand.

"We're old friends," she told me. "I've been feeding him sugar almost every night, when you were asleep." She patted his head. "You're a big, beautiful boy, aren't you?" she asked him. He nuzzled her hand. He obviously liked her, which was rare for the big horse. He had always been a one-man horse—but then, Sara was a woman.

A fact I suddenly became acutely aware of.

"C'mon," I told her. "We've got to build a fire."

"From what?" she asked, "stones?"

"No, but we'll use them, too." I gathered up some brush that was growing up from between the rocks. "Round stones," I told her. "Gather them up and put them in a circle."

She picked up a small one and said, "Like this?"

"No," I told her, picking up one the size of an apple, "like this."

She gathered the stones and put them in a circle. I brought the brush over and put it inside the circle, then moved the stones to reduce the size of the circle. Using two of the stones I started a small fire, one that would heat the stones while it burned. If we ran out of brush for the fire, we could put the heated stones beneath the bedroll.

"C'mon," I told her. We sat by the fire and wrapped the blanket around both of us.

"This is not too bad," she told me.

"I guess not," I said. I could feel her body heat right through her clothing, and her breasts pressing against my arm.

"In fact," she said, placing her hand inside my shirt, "it could get better."

I felt the erection growing between my thighs, but first I wanted to talk.

"Sara, wait," I told her, grabbing her hand.

She seemed to know why I wanted her to wait, and she dropped her hand.

"I can't answer any questions, Clint."

"Well, that's too bad, because I've got a million of them."

"I know you do, and you deserve answers—"

"I'm getting tired of being told that. First by Kate, now you. I deserve some answers, but nobody is giving me any. Why is that?"

She looked into the fire.

"Oh, I'm sorry, that was a question, wasn't it? Oops, so was that."

"Clint, please—"

"Okay, okay, dammit!"

I pulled her to me and kissed her. I was going to have to work out my frustration somehow, and it seemed better than beating her up.

Her tongue leaped into my mouth and her hands became busy with my pants. We fell backward and the blanket opened beneath us. In no time at all we were completely naked and totally unaware of the cool mountain breeze.

Her skin was incredibly hot, burning hot to the touch.

Her hands began teasing me, bringing me to an unbelievable hardness.

"It's almost like smooth stone," she cooed, sliding down to take my smooth stone into her hot mouth.

She was in total control, and I was surprised to find myself perfectly willing to let her be. She did incredible things to me, things no eighteen-year-old girl should have known how to do. Her nails and fingers played with my testicles, while her lips, tongue and teeth did things to my penis that made it swell almost to bursting —and then refused to let it burst. She had me squirming on that blanket, silently begging for release.

Suddenly I became very angry, even more angry than I had been just moments before, when I wasn't getting any answers to a wealth of questions I had.

I grabbed her shoulders roughly and she protested, "Hey."

"Up," I told her.

She resisted and I forced her up and onto her back.

"Clint—"

"Keep quiet," I told her.

"Clint, I don't like this—"

"Why, because you're not in control now?" I asked, pinning her with my weight. "You control men, don't you, Sara? You're not the sweet young thing you're supposed to be. You controlled me at the stream that day, and my guess is that our blonde friend, Lam, has also spent some time under your control. Well, not this time, lady. This time I get to be in control."

I kissed her hard, hard enough to bruise her lips. I remembered she liked it rough, but she had still been in control that time.

Not this time.

She struggled, and fought, but her struggling became weaker and weaker, and finally ceased. I used my hands and my mouth to tease her this time, to bring her to the brink of exploding, and then denying her.

"Oh, God, Oh, Jesus! Clint. Oh, oh, *oh!*"

We went on like that for a while, and still I wouldn't let her climax.

"Oh Jesus, Clint, don't . . . don't make me . . . wait . . ."

But I did. I made her wait, and wait, and wait . . . and then I let her go.

She screamed, and it echoed off the mountains. I spread her legs wide and rammed myself home, and she went into an uncontrolled frenzy, bucking, writhing, panting—and cursing, saying things in my ear no eighteen-year-old girl should know about.

But then Sara was no mere eighteen-year-old girl.

But what was she?

Oh, I'm sorry, that was another question.

Wasn't it?

21

It was quite a night on that mountain, but come morning Sara still wasn't answering any questions. We huddled together for warmth, and the next time we made love nobody was in control. We shared the experience. No one made love *to* anyone, we made love *with* each other.

When we woke she was quiet, even meek. She went over and cooed to Duke while I broke camp and then saddled him up.

"Where are we headed?" she asked.

"You tell me," I told her.

"You mean—"

I buckled my gunbelt on, and slid my rifle back in its scabbard.

"I mean I'm going to finish the job I'm getting paid for. I'm going to take you wherever it is you're supposed to go—but this time, no blindfold."

"They'll take your gun away again, Clint."

"Maybe so, but I'm going to hold you to your word."

"What do you mean?"

"You said you wouldn't let anything happen to me?" I reminded her. "I guess now we'll see how good you are at keeping your word."

I mounted Duke and reached down to help her up.

"Clint?" she said, sliding her arms around me.

"What?"

"Would you believe me if I told you I think I'm in love with you?" she asked.

I thought of several ways to answer that, then decided to give her some of her own medicine. Besides, it would keep us from getting into a serious discussion on the matter.

"That's a question," I told her.

"So?"

"I'm not answering any questions right now."

We rode in silence for a while.

"Where are we going?" I asked after a few moments.

"When you get answers to all of your questions, will I get an answer to mine?" she asked.

"Yes," I said, without thinking.

"Okay."

She told me that in order to get where we were going we could either go down the mountain, and then around, or we could keep going up and over.

"It depends on how good Duke is," she added. "It's pretty rough going."

"You've been this route before, huh?"

"I've heard," she said, "that it's pretty rough going."

"We'll go over," I told her, then patted the big boy's neck and said, "Won't we, pal?"

"You love this horse, don't you?"

"That's a question," I reminded her, "but I'll answer it."

"You don't have to. I can see it plain as day. I wonder if, when you love a woman, you'll show it as openly."

I didn't reply to that.

I wondered, too.

As we rode, I wondered about the trip over the mountain. Lam had said he wanted to get where we were going by dusk of the day before. He wouldn't accomplish that by going all the way around the mountain.

Where was Sara directing me to?

I found out sooner than I expected. At noon, to be exact, when we got to the top.

"That way," she said, pointing to the left.

"Down is that way," I told her, pointing down.

"We're not going down," she told me.

"Where are we going then?"

She pointed again and repeated, "That way."

I wheeled Duke to the left and we went that way. We rode along the top for a while, then hit a decline. Little by little, the decline changed and then, suddenly, we were in a small valley.

And then I understood.

I'd had a hunch, ever since Baxterville, and it had gotten stronger and stronger as we went along. The refusal of Sara and Kate—and even Billie—to answer questions about our destination. Kate's guilt over that night in Anadarko. Her loyalty to a man who was dead.

Or was supposed to be dead.

"Right there, Mister," a voice called out, breaking into my reverie.

I stopped Duke and showed whoever it was my hands. He couldn't see Sara because she was behind me. But he could hear her.

"Ease up, Roy," she yelled out. She slid from the saddle to the ground and stepped forward so he could see her.

"Sara," the voice called out. He stepped out of hiding then, where I could see him. He was a short, squat guy holding a rifle in his folded arms.

"We was worried about you. Heard you got separated

when the Apaches hit."

"Let us through, will you, Roy?" she said.

"Sure, go on. They'll be glad to see you."

Sara said to me, "Slide down, Clint, and let Duke walk. It's not far."

"Sure."

I dismounted and followed her. I had noticed something when we reached the top of the mountain and she changed directions on me. I was even more aware of it now. She'd changed from that point on, and now she was like a different person.

I was starting to think that maybe I'd made a mistake, walking right back into the rattler's lair when I'd been lucky to get out once.

"Is this what I think it is?" I asked Sara. We'd come into site of some wooden shacks, and there were men milling around, some working, some just standing around, talking and laughing. It looked almost like a small town, hidden away here in the mountains.

"What do you think it is, Clint?" she asked.

"I think this is where Con Macklin went when he died. This is Con Macklin's Heaven."

"The word is Haven," a voice said from behind me. I turned to face the man behind the voice.

He was a big man, not as big as the Apache I'd had to fight, but he exuded the same kind of arrogance and confidence. He was in his early or mid-forties and his broad face needed a shave. His eyes were mean. After all those years as a lawman, I knew mean eyes when I saw them, and Con Macklin had two of the meanest.

"But you've got the right idea," he added.

"Con Macklin."

"Hello, Con," Sara said.

"Hello, Sara, baby," he replied. "We missed you."

He stepped forward, took her in his arms and kissed

her roughly on the mouth.

Whatever else Sara was, at least this answered part of my question.

She sure as hell wasn't Con Macklin's daughter.

22

They took my guns and my horse and locked me in one of the shacks.

Macklin hadn't had to draw his gun. There were two men on the other side of me with their guns already out and pointing at me.

"The belt, pal," Macklin told me. Take it off."

I took it off, then waited to be told what to do with it.

"Take it, Sara."

"Con—"

"Take it!" he snapped, and she jumped. She was afraid of him, that was easy to see. Even when he was kissing her I could see that she was afraid of him.

"Here," I told her, holding it out. She took it, thanking me with her eyes.

"Put him in a shack," Macklin told his men. "I'll talk to him later."

So they stuck me in a shack with a table, a chair and a cot. Not even a deck of cards to occupy my time. The windows were boarded up, so I couldn't see out, and I had no light. There was a lamp, though, and some matches. I guess they weren't afraid I'd burn the shack down. If I did, they'd probably just put me in another one, and without a lamp.

I sat on the cot, listening to the sounds outside. I had

no conception of time, but pretty soon my stomach started telling me it was dinner time. My stomach turned out to be pretty reliable, because at that moment the door to the shack opened, letting in what was left of the light outside. Billie walked in, carrying a tray of food.

"Well, well, the other Macklin daughter who isn't a Macklin daughter."

She made no remark, simply set the tray down on the table. I got up from the cot and grabbed her arm.

"Billie—"

"There's a man outside. I can call him." She said it without emotion, just a simple statement of fact. I let go of her arm and shrugged.

She started for the door, then turned and said, "Kate will be in soon, Clint, to—to explain."

"Fine. I'll wait."

She frowned, and walked out. I was hungry and the food looked good, so I sat at the table and began to eat with gusto. Whatever was in store for me was going to happen soon enough. There was nothing I could do about it locked up the way I was, and there was no point in letting it spoil my appetite.

I finished the food and went back to sit on the cot. I began to feel drowsy, so I lay back and in a few moments I was asleep. I was awakened by the sound of the door opening.

It was Kate.

"You come to get the tray, it's on the table. Next time, the meat could be a little rarer. Speak to the cook, will you?"

She closed the door behind her, and I heard it lock from the outside.

"I didn't come for the tray, and I didn't come to talk about the food."

She was wearing a high-necked, yellow dress. Her large breasts strained the material, and her red hair was down around her shoulders.

"Dresses suit you," I told her, "and you should wear your hair down more often."

She shook her head and smiled.

"You sure can talk, Clint. I came to explain."

"What's to explain? You're probably no more Macklin's wife than Sara and Billie are his daughters. Or are those even their names?"

"Our names are real enough."

"Yeah, well, you may not be his wife and daughters, but I guess that doesn't make you any less his women."

"I guess not, and I won't apologize for that. Con Macklin took care of me, of us—"

"And shared you with his men?"

She looked down at the floor for a few moments, then lifted her chin up high and said, "Yes, maybe even that, but where would I be without Con Macklin?"

"Maybe better off," I told her, "but that's for you to decide."

"You're damned right it is," she snapped angrily. She turned her back and I saw her shoulders rise and fall, as if she were taking a deep breath to relax herself. When she'd regained her composure, she turned back.

"There's nothing to explain now, Kate. I can figure it out. You needed to get to Macklin and you couldn't do it alone. You needed help, and I hired on." I dug into my pocket. "I guess you'll want your two hundred dollars back."

"No. You'll get the rest of your money, I promise."

"Does Macklin promise?"

She didn't answer.

"Face it, Kate. He's going to kill me. I know where his little hideout is. He must be planning something big. He's got enough men here to build his own army."

"I'll talk to him. He won't kill you."

"Don't feel guilty."

"I don't!" she snapped. "He won't kill you," she said again, "I'll talk to him. You'll see."

She walked up to me, put her arms around my neck and kissed me. "You'll see," she said again. She picked up the tray, then thought better of it and put it down again.

"I'll tell them you weren't finished."

"Why?"

"It'll give Sara a reason to come in later," she told me.

Maybe she was going to come for the answer to her question.

When Kate left, I sat down and pondered it.

23

There wasn't a hell of a lot else to do, so I went back to the cot and went to sleep. Once again, I was awakened by the opening of the door.

As Sara stepped in, I could see that it was now pitch black. She shut the door behind her and it locked. She went to the table, grabbed the chair and took it back to the door. Obviously not wanting us to be interrupted, she jammed the back of the chair underneath the doorknob. Now the door was effectively locked from either side.

"Hello, Clint."

I sat up on the cot. "Hi, Sara."

"Are you all right?"

I raised my hands and replied, "Never better."

"Sure."

She walked across the room with her hands behind her.

"Did you get your answers from Kate?" she asked.

"A few. I figured out most of it. The rest will have to come from Con Macklin himself."

"Like what?"

"Like why did he give up Macklinville, turn it over to Dade Whitman, and let everyone think he was dead?"

"I can answer that," she told me, sitting on the other end of the cot.

"Oh?" I asked, feigning great surprise. "Are you willing to answer questions now?"

She shrugged.

"No reason not to."

"Okay, so why?"

"Con's set his sights higher than just owning a town. He got bored in Macklinville, so he contacted his friend, Dade Whitman, and told him he'd turn the town over to him if Whitman would help Con appear dead."

"I wasn't aware that Dade and Macklin were friends, but knowing Dade, I can understand it. What's this new ambition of Macklin's, that he needs an army for?"

She thought it over a moment, and I remembered she was afraid of Con Macklin, but that fear seemed to exist only when he was present.

"He wants to be President of Mexico."

I was stunned into silence.

"That's the way Kate reacted."

"President of Mexico," I repeated. "He's going to take on the whole Mexican army?"

"He wants to go right into the capital and take it over. He's got enough men to do it, too."

"He's got to have enough money to outfit them, though. Where does he—wait a minute!"

That was it! There *was* a treasure, and Macklin needed it to train, pay, and outfit his private army. Who knew how much money he'd amassed during the time he owned Macklinville—and towns before that?

"The treasure," I said aloud. "We had it all along, didn't we?" I asked. "It was on the wagon the whole time!"

She nodded her head.

"All in cash, too," she told me.

"How much?"

She shrugged. "I don't know. Neither did Billie. Only Kate and Con know how much Con's saved. He's been thinking about this for a long time."

"I'll bet."

"Can he do it, Clint?"

I thought about it. Mexico wasn't that big a country and it had had its fair share of changes in leadership. A superior show of force was usually all it took to pull it off.

"Yeah," I told her, "I think he might just be able to do it. If he's got enough men—enough fighting men—he might be able to pull it off."

"He told Kate he'll marry her as soon as he makes it."

"You don't believe him, do you?"

"No, I don't. Kate's always been his favorite, but lately he seems to prefer me. I didn't want to say anything to Kate." She laughed shortly. "I don't think she would have believed me anyway."

She moved closer to me on the cot.

"I'll use that, though, to make sure that Con doesn't hurt you, or kill you."

I put one arm around her and said, "You look out for yourself, Sara. I can take care of myself."

"How?"

"I have a couple of ideas, don't worry."

She put her head on my shoulder and asked, "Now that all your questions are answered, how about answering mine."

"What was it?"

"Okay, play it dumb, but I'm in love with you, Clint Adams. I want to know if you love me."

I decided to answer her honestly.

"No, Sara, I don't love you. I like you an awful lot, in spite of the fact that you lied to me. I think we can have a lot of fun together, but I don't love you. I'm sorry."

She was quiet a moment, then I thought I heard her laugh.

"Honesty from a man," she remarked, "that's something I'm not used to." She looked up at me and added, "I appreciate it, I really do."

I leaned over and kissed her gently at first, then with more urgency. Her arms went around my neck and her full body pressed up against me.

"What about Lam?" I asked.

She shrugged. "You have to latch onto somebody, Clint. Kate got Con, I took Lam." She kissed me lightly and whispered, "I'm not interested in Lam anymore."

Her hands went to the buttons on my shirt and slid inside.

"How was Billie?" she asked.

"What?"

"Billie, how was she?"

"You knew?"

She laughed.

"We agreed before the trip that we'd each try you out, then we compared notes. How was she?"

"She was good, very good, but I like my woman full-bodied," I told her, opening her shirt and cupping her breasts. I pushed her back on the cot and began kissing her breasts.

"You don't have to force me this time, Clint. You're the boss," she whispered, holding my head tightly against her breasts, "you're the boss."

I removed her clothing and dropped them on the floor. Then I stood up and removed mine while she watched. She reached out and stroked my erection lovingly.

"Will you try to escape?" she asked as I spread myself on top of her.

"Maybe. I haven't decided yet."

Her arms went around me and her nails played along my spine. She reached down and cupped my buttocks and began moving her hips beneath me.

"If you go, take me with you. Please?"

"You're sure you want to go?"

"I want to leave, Clint. I'm tired of being passed from man to man like a bottle of whisky, on Con Macklin's say-so. Lam's afraid of him, Kate's afraid of him, I'm afraid of him. You, you're not afraid of him." She wrapped her legs around me and I slid right into her easily. She caught her breath.

"You're not afraid of anybody. If Con knew what we were doing right now, he'd have you killed on the spot."

I kissed her deeply, then told her, "I couldn't think of a better reason to die."

24

Sara left and took the tray with her. I told her to tell Macklin that I wanted to talk to him. This time, when I hit the cot I knew no one would wake me up until morning, and if Macklin was going to talk to me, it would be tomorrow. If I was going to present my case well enough to gain his interest, I'd need a good night's sleep.

In the morning Billie came with my breakfast.

"Can we cut the shy act, Billie? I know all about you and Sara, and Kate."

She put the tray down on the table with a bang and turned to face me angrily. It was the first time I had seen an outward sign of emotion—other than the night we had had sex, and I couldn't say for sure that she had felt any legitimate emotion that time, either.

"You know all about me, huh?" she demanded. "Well I got news for you, Mr. Clint Adams. You don't know nothing about me. I do what I do for a reason, and I don't have to explain anything to you. As far as my being shy, being a whore doesn't mean I can't be shy, you know. Don't go judging me!"

"Billie, take it easy, I'm not judging you, just like I'm not judging Sara or Kate. I thought we might be friends."

She shook her head. "Sara's the one who wants to be

friends with you, Clint. She loves you. If you leave here, take her with you. She doesn't belong here anymore."

"And you do?"

"Maybe I don't, but I'll leave when I'm ready, and on my own," she told me. She started to leave.

"Wait a minute."

She turned.

"Did Sara tell Macklin I wanted to talk to him?"

"Yes. He's going to come by later."

I nodded.

"Okay, thanks."

"They've both been talking to him," she told me. "Kate and Sara, both trying to get him not to kill you."

"And you?"

She laughed.

"Me? What influence would I have on him? I'm only his real daughter and he still passes me around, just like Sara and Kate. What influence could I possibly have?" she said, bitterly.

I had to agree with her.

25

Macklin kept me waiting until after lunch, which was also delivered by Billie. When she came to pick up the tray, he came with her.

"Just pick up the tray and get out, girl," he growled at her. She did as he said without once looking over at me. When she was gone Macklin closed the door and stayed in the room with me alone. Obviously he wanted to show me that he wasn't afraid of me.

He took the chair from next to the table, reversed it and sat down, arms resting on the back of the chair. He was wearing his gun, and if I could have overcome him and gotten his gun I might have had a chance to escape. All I'd have to do after that is fight my way through an army of armed men.

Simple.

"You wanted to talk to me?"

"I want to know what the story is, Macklin. How long do you expect to keep me here? What do you intend to do with me?"

"Well," he said, sticking his little finger in his ear and scratching vigorously, "I been thinkin' about that one myself."

"And?"

"I'm havin' a hard time. You see, my first thought

was to kill you. Then Kate started talkin' for you, sayin' how you helped her and all, and Sara started talkin' for you, saying the same things. Seems you really impressed those two women of mine."

He wasn't finished, so I just waited.

"Who do you figure was after you?" he asked me.

"They weren't after me, Macklin, they were after your money."

"You knew about my money?" he asked.

"I knew there was talk about it, but I didn't know whether to believe it or not. I certainly didn't know that the money was in the wagon the whole time."

"So, who was after my money?" he asked again.

"I think it was Dade Whitman," I told him.

"Whitman?" he said, startled. "Whitman's a friend of mine. I gave him my town."

"Macklin, I've known Dade Whitman for a long time—"

"So've I."

"Then you know that Dade Whitman's only friend is Dade Whitman," I told him.

He was thinking about it, so I went on.

"One of the men I killed was a man named Shagan."

"I know Shagan."

"Well, Whitman was going to make Shagan one of his deputies."

He rubbed the bristles on his jaw with his big hand.

"You might be right, Adams."

"You know I'm right."

He grunted and stood up, putting his hands on his hips.

"You're smart," he told me. "I could use a smart man. Kate tells me you're good with a gun. Sara says you made your own gun. Is that true?"

"It's true."

"Your name rings a bell with me. Why's that?"

"I was a lawman for a while, up North. I worked with Hickcock some—"

"And you make your own guns," he muttered, as if it had just come to him. "Ain't you the lawman they called the Gunsmith?"

"I've been called that, yes."

He slapped his knee.

"Well, I'll be damned," he said, and started laughing. "I will be damned!"

Laughing the whole time, he turned and walked to the door. Shaking his head he opened it and started to walk out.

"Hey, Macklin—"

Still laughing he turned and waved a hand at me.

"I'll be back soon, Adams. I got to think on this some more." He was still laughing when he shut the door behind him.

26

Next time the door opened it was still light out and the blonde man, Lam, stepped in.

"Let's go," he said. His gun wasn't in his hand, but his hand was dangling down near it. I had no doubt but that he could get that gun to clear leather quick enough.

I got up from the cot and asked, "Where are we going?"

"Con wants to see you."

He let me walk out first, and the sun assaulted my eyes. Judging from its position, it was after three.

"What's your last name, Lam?" I asked him. We walked across the compound to one particular structure that was better built than the rest.

"Why do you want to know that?" he demanded.

I shrugged. "Idle curiosity."

He was behind me, so I couldn't see his face. He waited a few moments, then I guess he decided there was no harm in answering.

"James," he said, and then gave me a little push. He was intent on keeping us from becoming friends, but he needn't have worried about that.

We entered the building he had directed me to and I found that it was set up as a saloon. There was a complete, well-stocked bar and a bartender. In the middle of the room sat Con Macklin at a table, with his arm around Kate. She was wearing a fancy, brightly-colored dance hall dress. Sara, similarly dressed, was seated across from them. Billie was nowhere in sight.

"Sit down, Adams. Want a drink?" Macklin asked.

"I could use one," I told him. I took the only seat available, next to Sara. She sneaked me a look, hoping Macklin wouldn't see her do it.

"Get him a drink, Sara," he told her.

She got up without a word and went to the bar to get me a drink.

"Hell, bring the whole bottle," he yelled over to her. It was obvious that he'd had a few drinks already. I looked behind me and saw that Lam had taken up a position right by the door, keeping his eye on me.

Sara came back to the table with a bottle of whisky and a glass. She poured the whisky out for me, then sat back down.

"Adams, I told you this before. You're a smart man. On top of that, you're good with a gun. I could use you, for both reasons." He finished his drink and poured out another. "I've got a few men who are pretty good with their guns, but none of them are smart. That includes Lam, over there. He knows how to follow orders, but he ain't smart."

"Wait a minute—" Lam broke in.

"Shuddup!"

Lam came forward, shouting, "You can't talk to me like that. Not in front of—of him," he said. What he really meant was, not in front of Sara.

"Get outta here, boy," Macklin told him, his tone low and menacing. Lam James's gun-hand was twitching, but I knew from his eyes that he wasn't going to pull his gun. Things stayed frozen that way for a few moments, then the younger man turned and stalked out.

"Gotta keep them in line, you know what I mean?"

Macklin asked, laughing and downing another drink. I drank about half of mine. It felt good, burning its way down my throat, but I didn't intend to drink too much of the stuff. I was going to need my wits about me if I intended to get out of there alive.

"So," Macklin snapped, pouring himself another drink, "I got room for you, Adams."

"Doing what?"

"Doing what you do best, working with guns. Showing my men how to use 'em, how to take care of 'em, repairin' what needs to be repaired."

"What's in it for me?" I asked.

He leaned forward with his drink in his hand and peered at me through glassy eyes.

"You don't get killed," he said, then laughed uproariously.

"I've got some money coming to me," I told him. He stopped with his drink halfway to his mouth.

"You got guts, I'll say that," he told me. He finished his drink, put down the glass and dug in his pocket. He came up with a wad of bills and threw it on the table.

"There's more there than you got comin'."

I reached over and counted out two hundred.

"I'll just take what I've earned—so far," I told him, tucking the money away in my shirt.

He shook his head and took back what was on the table.

"There's more where that came from. You stay here and work for me, you don't get killed plus you get rich. What do you say?"

I emptied my glass and poured another drink for myself. I held the glass up to him and said, "Just so long as I don't have to go back to that shack," and drank it down.

He laughed and poured himself another drink. The level of the liquid in the bottle was decreasing fast, and most of it was due to him. He could hold his liquor. His eyes were glassy, but I knew his mind was still sharp.

"You can have a room upstairs. Sara will show you where it is." He looked at her and she nodded. "Later, though. First we're gonna eat."

As if on cue a man with an apron came out of a back room with a tray of food. There were two plates on it, and he set one in front of me and the other in front of Macklin.

"I'll need my guns," I told him.

"Nah," he disagreed, "you won't need them. There's lots of armed men around here. You'll be safe, don't worry. Maybe later on, you'll get your guns. Right now, eat. After we eat you can go upstairs and Sara'll take care of you," he added, winking at me. "Only, don't get used to it. We share the women around here, Adams. Draw lots in the morning to see who gets 'em at night. I held Sara aside for you tonight. Wanted to show you that I can be good to my men."

I tasted the food and he went on.

"Good food, good booze, good women," he told me. He looked at Kate and then reached over and fondled her breast. "Damned good women, too. Maybe one of these nights I'll let you have Kate, here." He patted her shoulder. "She don't always go into the draw, you know. She's my favorite."

Kate smiled at him and touched his hand, but I thought she looked embarrassed.

"Then again, I can be mean too, Clint," he told me, leaning over his plate. "I can be damned mean if I have to. I hope I never have to show you that side of me. You better hope I never have to show you that side of me."

The room got quiet all of a sudden and I was aware of Sara's breathing next to me.

"C'mon, then. Eat up," he said, breaking the silence. We ate up and he told Sara to get another bottle. I was careful about the amount of whisky I consumed, but after a while things started to get a little hazy. By the time we were finished there were other men in the saloon, drinking and playing cards. At one point I saw Billie come down from upstairs with a man, and then go right back up with another man. The look she gave me was a defiant one, as if to say she was doing what she was doing because she wanted to.

"C'mon, Kate," Macklin said as it got late. He grabbed her arm, staggered to his feet and hauled her up. "Let's you and me go on upstairs. Adams, Sara'll show you your room. You enjoy yourself, you hear? In the mornin' I'm gonna put you to work."

Leaning heavily on Kate, who looked as if she was used to it, he negotiated the steps to the second floor.

When he disappeared from sight, Sara put her hand on my arm.

"You going to stay and work for him?" she asked me.

I leaned over to her and said, "Not here. Pretend like I have to lean on you to get upstairs," I told her.

I staggered up on my feet and made as if I would have fallen if it hadn't been for Sara. There were some remarks thrown our way while we staggered up the steps. When we got to the top I stood up straight and asked, "Where's Macklin's room?"

She pointed to the right and said, "It's that last door at the end of the hall."

"And mine?"

She pointed to the left.

"He put you part of the way down there, on the left."

"C'mon," I told her, and started down the hall to my room.

Inside I was surprised to find how well furnished the room was. The bed was large and comfortable-looking. I looked out the window down at the empty compound. It was dark out by now and everyone was indoors.

"What do we do now?" she asked.

I turned to face her. Her breasts partially spilled from her gown, pushed up the way they were. The powder blue garment looked good against her fair skin and blond hair. I started unbuttoning my shirt and told her, "Right now I'm going to do just what Con Macklin said to do. Enjoy myself."

She smiled at me and reached behind her for the catch to her dress.

When we were both naked I looked at her for a few moments. Full, firm, wonderfully-rounded breasts, pink nipples already hardened with anticipation. She reached up, causing them to jut out towards me, and undid her hair, letting it fall to her shoulders like a golden waterfall.

A beautiful room, a gorgeous woman, a comfortable bed. What more could you want? I asked myself.

Freedom.

27

Afterward, with her head nestled against my shoulder, she asked, "How come you never asked about Duke?"

I laughed softly.

"You love that horse," I told her. "I knew you'd see that he was taken care of."

She wiggled against me and sighed comfortably.

"I told Con I wanted him for myself, and he said I could have him. He misses you, you know. I can tell."

"Yeah, well, we've been together a long time, me and the big boy," I told her. "Sara, where does Macklin have my guns?"

"In his room, I think. Locked up. After he talked to you he came back and asked me and Sara why we didn't tell him that you was the Gunsmith. I didn't know, and Kate said she didn't, either, although I think she did."

"She might have heard it in Anadarko," I told her.

"What does that mean?"

I shrugged.

"It's just a nickname I picked up, that's all. It doesn't mean anything."

"Con had a lot more respect for you after he talked to you, so it must mean a lot more than nothing."

I didn't answer.

"Why did you say that if Macklin knew about us last

night he'd kill me?" I asked. "He sent you up here with me, didn't he?"

"That's just it. He sent me up here, so it's all right. Last night, that was our idea. Macklin doesn't mind sharing us, as long as it's with his say so," she explained.

"What about Kate?"

"Sometimes he shares her, sometimes he don't. When he wants to be with me, he lets them draw for Kate in the morning. Sometimes even he draws, but he fixes it so he'll end up with me."

"Can't say I blame him," I told her. She reached up and kissed me lightly.

"Clint, what are you going to do?" she asked, suddenly concerned. "You're not really going to stay and work for him, are you?"

"For a while. There's got to be a way out of here, but I have to be free to move around first. I have to gain his confidence. If he thinks I've really joined him, he'll let up after a while, maybe give me back my guns." I paused a moment, then added, "That is, if the Federales don't find us first."

"What makes you say that?"

"If he's plotting to overthrow the present government, word's going to get around. You can't keep that kind of thing quiet. They're out there looking, all right. It's just a matter of finding this place before Macklin's ready."

I made her sit up so I could look right at her. She clutched the sheet a moment, then let it drop, revealing her big, pale globes.

"I want you to keep aware at all times," I told her.

"What for?"

"For trouble. If the Mexican army finds this place they'll ride in here and slaughter as many as they can before they take prisoners. If that happens, find me. Do you know another way out of this valley?"

"I've heard talk of one."

"Do you think you could find it?"

She thought a moment, then said, "I think so."

"All right. When the time comes we'll go that way, but if the Federales hit before we're even ready, find me and we'll try for it. Is that clear?"

She nodded and said, "Yes, it's clear. Hold me now?"

She climbed atop me and I held her tight.

"We'll get out of here," I promised her. "We'll get out."

"I know, I know," she whispered.

"Sara, does Macklin always treat Lam like that?"

"Yes."

"For a moment there Lam looked like he was going to go for his gun. Would he?"

"He's very fast," she told me, "but so's Con. I don't think Lam would ever try it, though."

"Why not? Is he afraid?"

She paused, and the pause grew longer.

"Sara?"

"He's not afraid, really," she finally said.

"Then what?"

She propped herself up on my chest and looked at my face.

"Lam is Billie's brother," she told me.

"You mean—"

She nodded. "He's Macklin's son."

28

The next day Macklin put me to work.

He showed me to a livery that was outfitted with everything a smithy would need. There were quite a few guns that were damaged that he had been waiting to have repaired.

"All these guns," I told him. "You trust me with them?"

He laughed.

"There's not a bullet in the place, Adams. Sure, with an empty gun, I trust you."

I picked them up and inspected them.

"Some of these things are old," I said. "Others are just neglected."

"That's what I need you for," he told me. "To make damned sure these men know how to treat their guns. How long will it take you to fix these?"

For the most part the problems were minor.

"Not long. By lunch, maybe."

"Okay. After lunch I want you to start talking to the men. I'll send them to you about five or ten at a time."

"How many have you got?" I asked.

"There are—" he began to answer, then caught himself and finished "—enough."

I didn't push the matter. It was too soon for him to

trust me. Besides, if I really wanted to know how many men he had, all I had to do was count them as he sent them to me.

For the next few weeks I felt like a teacher, holding classes every day on the care and handling of a gun. There were some wise guys in the camp, but for the most part the men were young, willing to learn. They realized the more they learned, the longer they'd stay alive.

They were leery of me at first, then gradually began to accept me. Again, there were a few who never would, and they were led by Lam. He seemed to have about six or eight men who watched his every move. If I was going to have trouble, it would come from him and his friends.

The evenings were mostly occupied by poker, for the men who weren't lucky enough to draw one of the women for the evening. I participated in the draw after the first two weeks, which was my first real sign of acceptance. That week I drew the winning straw once, and it was Sara. We laughed about it afterward, in bed. It was meant to be, she said. I didn't agree. Sara was becoming too dependent on me, and I hoped Macklin wouldn't notice. Whenever we were close her eyes were always on me. Kate noticed, but I didn't know if Macklin had.

Lam noticed, too, because he had eyes for Sara. It was obvious that Lam was Macklin's bastard son and that Lam resented him for that. It was also obvious, though, that there was a certain amount of respect, admiration and even affection that Lam felt for his father.

I couldn't say the same for Billie, though. I did notice that she seemed to have some feelings for Lam. I wondered if they had the same mother.

As far as Macklin was concerned, I knew Billie felt bitterness towards him, but I wondered if it went beyond that. I wondered if she actually hated him.

About three weeks after I first started working with the men, I had two run-ins with one of Lam's men. His name was Bart Lane, and he was about Lam's age, twenty-seven or so. He wore his gun down low and walked with a swagger. He didn't think there was anything I could teach him, and he never failed to let me know it.

One of the things I had tried to drum into every man's head was this: never draw your gun unless you intend to use it. There was entirely too much horseplay involving guns. One day I noticed Bart Lane continuously drawing his gun and putting it to someone's nose because they couldn't outdraw him.

I walked up behind him and as he went to draw on a kid about nineteen or twenty, I put my hand over his gun. He turned quickly and, when he saw it was me, he yelled, "Don't ever touch my gun!"

"How many times have I told you never to draw this goddamned thing unless you mean to use it?" I demanded.

We began a heated argument and a small crowd gathered. In the crowd I saw Con Macklin.

"You think you're really good with that, don't you, Lane?" I asked finally.

He raised his chin and looked around at the crowd. He shifted his gunbelt and said, "Yeah, I'm pretty good."

"Draw on me," I told him.

"You ain't gotta gun," he pointed out, laughing.

I stepped to within an arm's reach of him and told him, "That doesn't matter. Go ahead, do to me what you were going to do to the kid. Draw your gun and stick it under my nose."

He smiled, turned his head slightly to the side. He was going to try to throw me off.

"I'll stick it *up* your nose," he said. While his head was turned away from me he went for his gun. I let him grip the butt, then put my hand over his so fast he didn't realize it. He went to pull his gun and couldn't move his hand.

Everybody laughed and he turned red. He yanked his hand away and said, "What the hell!"

"Go ahead," I said, dropping my hand to my side. "Try it again."

He tightened his lips and looked around at the smiling faces of his friends. Macklin wasn't smiling, just watching intently.

He tried the same dodge, but he wasn't any more successful this time than the last. In fact it was worse, because I got to his gun first and pulled it out of his holster.

"Gimme my gun!" he shouted, reaching for it.

"Lane, if I catch you pulling this gun again for any reason other than using it," I said, waving it at him, "I'll stuff it up your nose."

"Give him a gun," he shouted, looking around. "Somebody give this smart ass a gun, dammit!"

Macklin stepped forward and all the noise stopped.

"Let me get this straight, Lane," Macklin said. "You wanna draw on this man?"

"I'll kill him, Mr. Macklin. He can't make fun of me."

"He can and he has, Lane, but O.K. You want it that way, that's the way it'll be."

He turned to me and said, "Give me his gun." I placed it in his outstretched hand. He turned and handed it to Lane. "Put it away." He turned to the crowd and said, "Clear out."

They scattered to where they could watch in safety.

"Come with me," Macklin told me. He walked me about twenty feet away from Lane, emptying his own gun as he went. He holstered his gun, removed the holster and handed it to me.

"You've got one bullet, Adams," he told me. "Make it count."

"Macklin—"

"This is the way the kid wants it, Adams," he told me. "And it's the way I want it."

I shrugged and accepted his gunbelt. I strapped it on and Macklin walked to the side.

"I'll say when," he told us both.

Lane was fidgeting from one foot to the other, rubbing his hands. He shook his gun hand around, loosening it up. I stood perfectly still, trying to think how to play it. I didn't want to kill him, but I only had one bullet. If I wounded him he could still kill me.

There was only one thing to do.

"Ready!" Macklin shouted.

"Go!"

I drew and fired. By the time Lane's hand got to his gun, it was gone.

I'd used my one bullet to sever his holster and gun from his belt. They were about ten feet behind him, in the dirt. The moment was followed by dead silence, then gradually the laughter began to build up. Lane, face red and eyes bulging, walked over to his gun and picked it up.

"That's it, Lane," Macklin yelled. "He bested you and it's all over."

Lane stood staring at me for a few seconds, then turned and stalked away.

I unbuckled the gunbelt and handed it back to Macklin.

"Why didn't you kill him?" Macklin asked. "That was pretty fancy shooting."

"Fancy hell," I told him. "I was aiming for his navel."

29

That same night I was playing poker when Lane walked into the saloon. There was an empty chair at the table. I was holding the deck.

"Room for one more?" he asked me, since I was dealing.

"Suit yourself," I told him.

He sat down and I dealt out the cards.

I was slightly ahead at that point, but from then on Lane got hot. After a couple of hours he was way ahead and loving every minute of it.

"Let's get some drinks," he said to Billie, who was standing by.

"Not me," I told her. I didn't drink while I was playing cards.

When she brought him his drink he put his arm around her waist and said, "You and me later, baby. I won the draw."

She smiled wanly at him, then looked at me with those big, defiant doe's eyes.

As he kept drinking Lane started to lose. Gradually he lost his winnings and then he was in the hole.

I dealt out what was to be the final hand of the evening. The game was seven-card stud. There were five of us left in the game.

Lane was high man on the table with a king. I had a six showing, and two more in the hole.

"Twenty dollars," Lane said cockily. He was so cocky, in fact, that I felt sure he had another king in the hole, maybe two. It was going to be an interesting hand.

One player dropped out, and the rest of us called. I dealt again. Lane got himself a queen, I got a five, which didn't help. One of the other players received an ace, however, so Lane wasn't high on the table anymore. The ace bet ten, and when it got around to Lane he raised twenty. Everyone went out except me and the man with the ace. I noticed that one of the men who folded did so with his first card, which was low, and his second, which was a king. I thought sure that Lane hadn't noticed that a king was gone. That meant the most he could hope for now was kings full.

I dealt the next card.

Lane got another queen, which made him rub his hands with glee. I decided to play him as if he had the full house. The second man paired his aces and decided to go ahead and bet.

I got another five, which gave me a full-house, with three sixes over the fives.

A very good hand, but it still could end up second- or even third-best.

The aces bet twenty dollars. I raised, and Lane raised me. Now it was forty dollars to the aces and he was tentative about staying in, but did so. He didn't have anything better than aces. I called Lane's raise.

The next card didn't help any of us. The aces checked, and so did I. Lane cackled and bet forty dollars. The aces folded, but I called.

I dealt out the last card, feeling sure that Lane already had his full-house.

I looked at my last card and didn't allow anything to show on my face. Lane, on the other hand, was drunkenly laughing up a storm, showing his hand to all of his friends who'd gathered behind him.

I was high on the board with five, now that the aces had gone out.

"A hundred dollars," I told him, and pushed it into the center of the table. That got the attention of everyone else in the room, including Sara, Kate, and Macklin.

Lane frowned, counting the money in front of him. He pushed a hundred dollars in and then said, "I wanna raise a hundred."

I looked in front of him where his money had been. There was nothing there.

"You don't have a hundred dollars," I told him.

He frowned and felt around with his hands, finally deciding I was right. "So," he snapped, "I'm good for it."

I shook my head.

"I don't play credit," I told him.

He started to get angry.

"They'll tell you," he snapped at me, waving behind him. "They'll tell you I'm good for it!"

"I don't care what they tell me," I informed him. "I don't play for credit."

"I wanna raise!" he shouted. He looked up at Billie, standing next to him.

I knew what he was going to say before he said it, and I'd already decided to accept it.

"Her!" he said, triumphantly. "I got her. I'll bet her. She's worth a hundred dollars, ain't she?"

I looked at Billie, who stared right back at me.

"Yeah, I guess she is. Okay," I said, pushing another hundred dollars into the pot. "I accept your raise."

He laughed out loud and turned his cards over.

"Kings full," he said, then repeated, "full house, kings full. Hah, ha!"

He started to reach for the money and I put my hand over his.

"No good," I told him.

"The hell it ain't," he snapped. He pointed to the man who'd had the aces on the table. "He folded two aces, so you ain't got aces full. My hand's good. Take your hands off my money!"

"Kings full is second best, Lane," I told him. I turned my cards over.

My last card had been the fourth six.

There was a sharp intake of breath throughout the room, and then Lane tried to jump across the table at me, sending the money flying. A couple of his friends grabbed him and held him back.

"Put him in the shack for tonight," Macklin instructed, stepping forward. They took him out, I assumed, to spend the night where I had spent my first few days.

I picked up my money from the table and the floor, then stood up.

"I'm going to take my winnings and retire," I told Macklin. I reached over and took the half a bottle of whisky that was also sitting on the table, and started for the steps.

"Hey," Macklin called out.

"What?" I asked, turning. He pushed Billie and she stumbled into me.

"You forgot some of your winnings," he told me, grinning lewdly.

I looked down at her, but she was glaring at him.

"Yeah," I remarked. "I guess I did."

I took all of my winnings and went up to my room.

30

"You hate him, don't you?" I asked her.

She was lying with her head on my chest. We were both breathing hard and covered by a light sheen of perspiration. For a little girl she had an enormous amount of sexual energy.

"Yes," she answered.

"Then why don't you leave?" I asked her.

She picked up her head and looked at me.

"And go where?"

"Get your brother to go with you," I suggested.

"Lam? He's my half-brother."

"He hates your father too, doesn't he?"

"Don't call him that," she snapped angrily. "Don't call him my father."

"Sorry."

"Lam only hates him sometimes," she told me. "I hate him every minute of every day. With Lam it's part hero-worship, part hate, and part love. Lam wants to have a father so bad," she said, shaking her head.

I stayed quiet a while, playing with her hair. Her breathing became very even and for a minute I thought she had fallen asleep. Then I felt her eyelashes flutter against my chest.

"Billie?"

"Hmm?"

"If and when I leave, would you want to come with me?"

She paused a moment, as if thinking about it before answering.

"When are you leaving?" she finally asked.

"I didn't say I was, I said if I do."

"Well, if you do, is Sara going with you?"

"Yes."

She picked up her head again.

"Do you love her?" she asked.

"No."

"She loves you."

"So I've been told."

She moved up so she could reach my mouth with hers. Her tongue began to lash wildly around the inside of my mouth and her hand snaked to grip me. I started to get hard again, which was amazing to me.

"I'll come with you," she said between kisses.

She moved her hips and impaled herself on me. It was like a replay of that night in Texas. She was doing it practically by herself. Her eyes were shut tight and she was biting her lip so hard I thought she would bite right through. When she came she kept herself from shouting by covering my mouth with hers. I came just after she did, and only then did she stop riding me and relax.

"Lam loves Sara, you know," she told me.

"I figured that out."

"He's not going to like it if she leaves with you," she added.

"I really don't care what he likes," I told her.

"I hate him."

"Why?"

"He raped me once, when I was younger."

I didn't know what to say to that.

"It wasn't so bad, really. Just like any other man. After all, he's only my half-brother."

"Sometimes I think I'm sick," she told me.

"Why?"

"Because I like sex so much."

"That's not sick," I assured her.

She sat up and began to get dressed.

"Where are you going?"

"Bart didn't have me for the whole night," she told me, pulling her dress over her head.

I sat up.

"How many men do you have to see a night?" I asked her, remembering all the times I'd seen her come down with one man and then go right back up with another.

She shrugged, checking her appearance in a small mirror hanging on the wall.

"Sometimes, three, maybe four."

"Maybe more?"

She shrugged again.

I began to understand. She didn't just like sex, she needed it. No wonder she went wild.

"Maybe ten, or more?" I said.

She walked to the door and opened it, stopped when she was halfway out.

"I've had more," she confessed. She shrugged again and said, "I told you, I'm sick."

She left. I lay back with my hands behind my head.

I guess maybe it was a kind of sickness.

31

Three days later I drew straws in the morning for Kate, and I won. That meant that Macklin was going to spend the night with Sara. That would give me a good chance to talk to Kate without Macklin seeing us. I'd been waiting for a chance like that for a while.

It was up to the man who drew the winning straw to let the woman know. He could do it in the morning, or he could wait for the evening. I wasn't sure if Macklin always knew who the winner was. If he considered Kate his, he might make a point of knowing when he threw her up for grabs. I let her know early, in my own way.

I stopped into the saloon for a drink that afternoon, and I had the short straw in my mouth. When I caught her eyes I very deliberately touched the straw with my right hand. She gave me a small nod to show that she understood. I had one drink and then back out.

I had made a point of seeing Duke every day, to make sure the big boy was O.K. I went over to him now to brush him down and found Sara there, feeding him sugar.

"If he gets fat I'm going to blame you," I told her.

I startled her, but when she saw it was me she smiled. She was wearing a plaid shirt, jeans, boots, and had her hair in a pony tail. She looked very fresh and young.

"You know," I told her, touching her pony tail, "if I could let myself fall in love, it could very easily be with you."

She looked as if she were going to cry, but she managed to hold it back.

"Why can't you?" she finally asked. "Because I'm a whore?"

I grabbed her shoulders roughly and shook her.

"Don't be stupid!" I snapped at her.

"Then why?"

"Because I can't be tied down," I told her, dropping my hands from her shoulders. "It's as simple as that."

"I wouldn't tie you down, Clint."

"You wouldn't want to, Sara, but you wouldn't be able to help it. I'm sorry, but—"

"That's all right," she said quickly, touching her fingers to my mouth. "We can drop it—for now."

I smiled. "Okay, for now. Sara, how close are you with Billie?"

"Like sisters," she said without hesitation. "Like real sisters. Close enough so that she told me that when we leave she's coming with us." She touched my arm. "I'm glad you asked her, Clint."

"What about Kate?" I asked.

"Kate and I are friends. She's the closest thing to a mother I ever had. That's why I don't want to hurt her. I'm afraid Con's going to want me all the time and throw her out. That would kill her."

"You're going to be with him tonight, aren't you?"

"How did you know that?"

I showed her the short straw.

"I've got Kate." I dropped the straw and told her, "Listen, I want you to find out where he has my guns. We're going to need them when we leave."

"When are we going?" she asked, anxiously.

"Soon. There might be one problem."

"What's that?"

"Lam. He's in love with you."

She looked at the ground, shifted some hay around with her foot.

"I know, but I don't have any feelings for him. When we're together . . . in bed . . . sometimes he cries. He says he loves me and he'll take me away from here, but then the next day he's forgotten all about it. He'll never leave here."

"Why not? He doesn't love his father that much, does he?"

She shook her head.

"But he's tied to him. I don't know how, but he is. He wouldn't be able to live somewhere without him. It's like Con is a part of him, or is deep inside of him and won't let him go."

"What would he do if he saw you trying to leave?"

"He'd try and stop me."

"And if he knew you were going with me?"

"He'd try and kill you."

"Okay."

I thought a moment, then decided.

"Sara, this is what we'll do. After tonight, we'll go the next time Con wants you. That morning, after you've been with him, it's going to be up to you to get me my guns. I'll have the horses saddled and waiting. I'll tell Kate tonight, you can tell Billie. We've all got to start hoarding small bits of food. Not enough so's anyone will notice, but enough to hold us for a few days after we leave here."

Something occurred to me and I asked her, "Has he ever wanted you two nights in a row?"

"No."

"Not yet. Okay, look, if he wants you any time this week, we won't go, but after that it will be the very next time. Got it?"

"I've got it."

She stepped close to me and kissed me deeply. I returned it with feeling.

"You better go now. I don't want Lam to come looking for you."

"Okay. I'll see you later."

When she left I spent some time with Duke, talking to him. Sometimes I think he really understands everything I say to him.

"We'll be out of here soon, big boy," I told him, patting his rump. "And we'll have some company."

Again.

32

I waited until Macklin went upstairs with Sara before I nodded to Kate.

I went to the bar for a drink and put my key down on the top of it. When I finished my drink, the key was gone and so was Kate. I went upstairs and walked into the room without knocking. She was in the bed, beneath the sheet, and it was obvious that she wasn't wearing anything.

"Hi," I said.

"Hello."

I started to undress.

"Doesn't this ring a bell?" I asked her.

She nodded. "Anadarko."

"Right."

"I really enjoyed that night, you know."

"I could tell."

"I never wanted you to know it."

I slid in bed next to her. Her skin was warm, smooth, and fragrant.

"I always knew," I told her. Her arms went around me and we kissed, lightly at first, then hungrily.

We made love gently the first time, slowly, savoring every moment, every movement. When she climaxed she cried into my mouth and I bit her tongue gently.

"That was good," she told me.

"This time you want me to know right away, huh?" I asked.

She laughed and said, "As if you needed me to tell you."

We lay together for a while in silence, comfortable with each other. Once I almost fell asleep.

Finally I broke the silence.

"Kate, I'll be leaving soon."

"I know," she replied.

"How? Billie? Sara?"

"No, I could tell, Clint. I've come to know you pretty well, I think. I knew you wouldn't work for Con. You were just waiting for the right time. I also figured Sara would go with you."

"And Billie?"

"I wasn't sure about Billie. She's a lot like Lam. She doesn't love Con—in fact, she might hate him more than anyone else—but she's got him inside of her. Is she going with you?"

"She says she is."

"While she was up here with you?"

"Yes."

After a moment she said, "I hope she sticks to that decision. She'd be better off away from here."

"What about you, Kate?"

She laughed without humor.

"I've thought about it from time to time."

"You deserve better. You know that."

"Do I?"

"Yes, you do. Con Macklin is not for you, Kate, not the way he treats you. Do you want to be the first lady of Mexico? Is that it?"

"Don't be ridiculous," she scolded me. "Even if he succeeded in pulling it off, I know he won't marry me. If he marries anyone it would probably be Sara."

"You know—"

"What? That he's starting to become more and more interested in Sara? Of course I do. That's been coming for some time. I saw it even before he did."

"Sara doesn't want to hurt you," I told her.

"I know that. Sara is really a very sweet girl. She's very much in love with you."

"I wish people would stop telling me that."

"Make you nervous?" she asked, laughing.

"You asked me a long time ago not to hurt her, Kate. I don't want to."

"I know you don't. You love her a little bit, too, even if you won't admit it."

I didn't say anything to that.

"Okay, we won't talk about it."

"What about Lam?" I asked.

"He's headed for disaster. If he knows that Sara is going to leave with you, you'll have to kill him. I think he's destined to die anyway."

"Macklin?"

"He keeps pushing and pushing the boy. I don't know how much longer Lam can take it before he bursts."

"Could he kill Macklin?"

"Not in a fair fight," she said positively. "He's not the man Con is, and that's what eats him so."

She began to shiver.

"I'm cold all of a sudden."

I wrapped my arms around her and held her close, trying to warm her.

"When are we going?" she asked very quietly. I smiled to myself, glad she'd decided to come.

"The old team, together again, huh?" I said. We both laughed, and then we kissed. I told her the plan I'd told Sara.

"I've heard of that back way. Between Sara and me I think we can find it," she told me.

"Good."

"I'll also try and find out where Con has your guns. If Sara can't get to them, maybe I can. Why did you set it up so that we'd leave after one of the nights he spent with Sara?"

"I wasn't sure you'd come," I told her.

"Weren't you?" she asked, and kissed me again.

"I didn't want to take anything for granted," I told her. "Since we've got it set up this way, we'll leave it. Okay?"

"Okay, you're the boss," she told me.

"No, this is going to be a team effort," I told her.

"I guess it will be."

"Kate?"

"Yes?"

"Can I count on Billie?"

"I think so. She's a little strange sometimes, but I think we can."

She rolled over and brought me with her so I was on top of her. As we kissed I couldn't help but think that if we had a weak link in our plan, it was Billie.

I hoped that link wouldn't snap on us.

33

Two weeks later I woke with a bad feeling in the pit of my stomach. I knew that this would be the day, and I didn't want it to be. It didn't sit right.

I went downstairs and found out that Kate was up for the draw and the fluttery feeling in my stomach solidified and settled in one place.

I ordered some eggs and coffee and then threw my name into the draw. I didn't feel lucky, and I wasn't.

Lam James was. He drew Kate. Bart Lane drew Billie, and I was reminded of the night he lost his draw to me in a poker game. Since that day we pretty much steered clear of each other, but he was carrying a grudge and I hoped he wouldn't end up taking it out on Billie.

The draw over, those of us who wanted breakfast sat down. Most of the men had accepted me, would play poker with me and listen when I talked about guns. None of them, however, had taken to having their meals with me. When I ate I usually ate alone, so that was the case that morning.

I was finishing up when Sara came down. She nodded to me, which I took to mean that her name hadn't been in the draw because she was going to spend the night with Macklin. The eggs went cold in my stomach.

This was the day we make our move.

I built up a pretty good supply of food on my own, things that wouldn't spoil while we were waiting. Combined with what Sara and Kate had stowed away, we should have enough to get us to the town, where we could restock and figure out where we were going. Or rather, where they were going. I was going back to Baxterville, to see Dade Whitman and to collect my rig. I'd have to drop the three of them off somewhere, and then it was up to them. Their best bet might be to stay together and head East, but that was going to be up to them. I'd get them away from here, but that was all the responsibility I wanted or would take.

I went outside and took a walk to the stable to check on Duke. I was hoping that the early-morning mountain air would dispel the bad feeling I had, the doubts about this being the right day to put our plan into effect.

It didn't. If anything, when I reached Duke I felt worse, but I knew we'd have to go through with it. If I called it off I might lose Sara, Kate or both. I needed them to find that back way out of this valley—Macklin's Valley.

I figured to go on with my day the way I usually did and turned to go out of the stable. Macklin was standing in the doorway, watching me.

"That's a mighty fine-looking horse," he told me. "I don't think I've mentioned it to you."

"You haven't."

"How long have you had him?"

"I raised him."

He nodded.

"You know, I gave him to Sara when I thought—well, when I had other plans for you."

"She told me."

"I'm sure, if you asked her real nice, she'd give him back to you. What do you think?"

"I think you're probably right."

He nodded again. He was just making conversation. He had other things on his mind.

"Are my men ready?" he asked.

"Ready as they'll ever be," I told him. "Are you sure you've got enough?"

I had counted over fifty, but that didn't include the seasoned gunmen he hadn't seen fit to send to me. He might have had close to seventy men, all told.

"I never told you why I needed all these men, did I?"

So that was it.

"I never asked," I told him.

"Yeah, I know," he said. He took out some fixings and rolled himself a cigarette. "I think maybe that's what's been bothering me," he told me.

"How long's it been bothering you?"

"Since the first time I offered you a job teaching my men. You never asked why."

Which had been an oversight on my part.

"To me that means you already knew. How did you know, Adams? Who told you?"

"I guessed."

He laughed.

"How could you—"

"You're training a small army in a small country. For what reason, to cross the border and take over Texas? You couldn't be that stupid. So what was the other alternative? Mexico. It wasn't hard, really."

He thought it over while finishing his cigarette. He flicked it away and it landed in a small pile of hay. There was still some burning ash and it started a small fire. I walked over and stamped it out.

"It seems your men aren't the only ones who still have some things to learn," I told him.

He ignored my remark and walked over to Duke. He

scratched the big boy's nose and patted his neck.

"I suppose I could accept your explanation for now," he said finally.

"Well, if you don't accept it you'll never be able to trust me, and if you can't trust me, Macklin, you might as well kill me."

He turned to face me, hand dangling by his gun. He was studying my face, and my life hung in the balance.

Finally he seemed to relax.

"Okay, Clint. I'll accept your explanation. Like I said before, you're a smart man, and a smart man figures things out, right?"

"I guess."

He started walking out of the stable, then stopped and held up one hand.

"I almost forgot," he said.

"What?"

"We're moving out tomorrow."

"Tomorrow?"

"Yeah, a couple of hours after first light. Come by my room in the morning and I'll give you your guns."

"Right, right," I told him, but my mind was racing. Our move had to be made at first light, as planned, only we wouldn't have as much time as I had hoped for. If they were going to move out tomorrow, our absence would be discovered much sooner than I had planned.

We wouldn't have that much of a head start to work with and we'd have to travel faster than I wanted to.

I hoped the women would be up to it.

34

I went through the day preoccupied, hoping no one would notice.

Everyone knew we were to be heading out in the morning, and they were on edge. For that reason no one questioned my mood, because it resembled theirs. They just figured I was as edgy as they were, for the same reason.

I spent the night in my room alone, thinking about Macklin with Sara, Lam with Kate, and Bart Lane with Billie. I hadn't had an opportunity to talk to any of them, so I'd have to break the news to them just before we left. I hoped that they would react all right. I didn't want anyone to panic.

I was up an hour before dawn, before anyone else. I went down to the livery to saddle Duke and three other horses. My stash of food was also in the stable. I had dug a hole in the floor and covered it with a stack of hay. Now I brushed the hay aside and looked at what I'd stored. We wouldn't be able to afford a pack horse, because that would sacrifice speed. For the sake of speed we were going to have to do some hungry traveling. We'd each have to take as much food as we could on each of our mounts, and then ration it.

I got the horses saddled just as first light started to

break. I settled down to wait for the rest of my party, hoping they'd make it. I hoped Sara wouldn't have any trouble getting my guns.

Kate was the first to arrive, carrying a small sack.

"Hi," she said, breathlessly. She was dressed for traveling: heavy shirt, jeans, high boots.

"Hi."

One word, that was all I said, and she sensed that something was wrong.

"What's wrong?"

"Didn't Lam tell you?" I asked.

"No. He seemed unusually tense, jumpy, but no, he didn't tell me anything."

I kicked at the ground a little bit.

"Clint?"

"They're moving out today," I told her.

"Today?" She thought about it. "We won't have as big a head start as we planned, will we?"

"No, we won't. We'll have to travel faster, and lighter than we planned."

She nodded pensively.

"You still want to go?"

"Yes."

"What about the girls?"

"Sara will go wherever you do, Clint," she assured me.

"And Billie?"

"I honestly don't know, Clint. I haven't had a chance to talk to her lately."

I nodded. Still the weak link, Billie was.

Sara was second to arrive, carrying my guns.

"You got them," I said, feeling excited in spite of myself. I grabbed them and inspected them. I would have liked time to clean them, but we couldn't afford it. I put my gunbelt on and slid the rifle into the scabbard on my saddle. Then I turned and kissed Sara.

"Thanks. Any problem?"

"Not really. He talks when he's drunk."

She handed me her sack of food. Without waiting for Billie I started dividing the food into four packs, one for each of us to carry.

"Did you bring any guns?" I asked.

Kate reached into her shirt and brought out that old Colt of hers. She also had another sack in her hand, but before I could ask her what it was, Billie came in. Her appearance caused both Sara and Kate to gasp.

Her face was bruised and cut, her mouth swollen. She walked as if something hurt her.

"What happened to you?" Sara asked, rushing to her.

"Lane. He got drunk and remembered what Clint did to him a couple of weeks ago. He took it out on me."

There was a light in her eyes, one that even outshone the light her eyes had when she was having sex.

"What happened?" I asked further.

"I killed him," she announced triumphantly, and that explained the new look in her eyes. A new thrill had put it there.

"We've got to get going," I told them. "Can you ride?" I asked Billie.

"I'll ride," she assured me.

"Let's mount up."

I helped Billie onto her horse and secured a sack of food to her saddle. When I secured all the food we could carry, we all mounted up. Kate was still carrying that other sack.

"What's in the bag, Kate?"

"Some personal stuff I didn't want to leave behind, that's all," she told me. She rode out and we followed her. Outside we found a surprise.

Lam James and about six of his friends were outside waiting for us. They'd formed a semi-circle around the stable doors. Now they closed in around us.

"You can all go," Lam said, "but Sara stays."

Sara looked over at me quickly, and then a resigned look crossed her face.

"Go ahead, Clint," she told me. "Take Kate and Billie."

"We're not going without you," Kate told her.

"Come with us, Lam. You don't belong here," Billie told her half-brother.

"Shut up," he snapped at her. "All I want is Sara. The rest of you can go."

"Stay put, Sara," I told her. I could only see four of them, and I'd probably be able to take them, but the two behind us would get me. Still, it was my only chance of getting out. If I stayed, Macklin would kill me. God only knew what he'd do to the women. No, there was only one way to play it.

"Adams, if she doesn't stay we're gonna kill you, and then she'll have to stay anyway."

"You got it wrong, Lam. If any of your men draws his gun, I'm going to kill you. I may end up dead, but so will you. It's your move, son."

"Don't call me that!"

I locked onto his eyes. I didn't think he'd make a play, but then his eyes told me I was wrong. I hunched my back muscles, tensing for a bullet. They'd get me, all right, but I'd make damned sure I took Con Macklin's bastard son with me.

I saw him go for his gun and knew I'd get to mine first, but before either one of us could clear leather, I heard a shot and he hit the dirt with a hole in his head.

There was a volley of shots following that one, and we all looked over at the direction they were coming.

"Federales!" one of the men yelled.

Sure enough there were Federales pouring into the valley, firing as they came. Two or three of Lam's friends also went down, and I felt a tug at my left sleeve.

"Sara, lead the way!" I shouted. The three of them had frozen and I had to shout at them again. "Dammit, let's go or we'll be massacred with the rest of them! Sara!"

She kicked her horse into action and we followed. The Mexicans were pouring in from that one direction, and we started riding in the other. Most of the men—hell, all of them except for the five with Lam—were still asleep, even Macklin. The shooting would wake them up, but they'd have no chance.

It looked like we had all picked the same day to make our move. Us, Macklin, and the Mexican government. In the ensuing confusion, I hoped that we'd be able to get away.

I also wondered, however, who had tipped off the Federales of Macklin's plans and location.

There was only one name I could come up with.

Macklin's friend, Sheriff Dade Whitman.

35

Once I'd established that the Federales weren't following us, we stopped for a rest.

"We're not camping," I told them, "we're just taking a breather. I want to take a look behind us."

Kate saw to the horses while I crept up on some rocks to take a look behind us. Sara climbed up beside me. Billie sat on the ground to nurse her wounds.

"How's your arm?" Sara asked, noticing the hole and the blood.

"It's just a scratch," I told her. The bullet had nudged me in passing, that was all. The bleeding had already stopped.

"It doesn't look like they're following us," she observed.

"No. I guess they were satisfied with what they got. They must figure three women and a lone man are no danger."

"All those men, caught while they were asleep," she remarked, shaking her head. "Will they kill them all?"

"A lot of them will wake up and go right for their guns," I told her. "It's a reflex. The Federales will shoot anyone they see with a gun. That's also a reflex."

"What about refusing to leave without me?" she

asked. "Was that a reflex?"

"That was stupidity," I told her. "I could have got killed and you would have had to stay anyway."

"Yes," she said, leaning over and kissing me on the cheek, "I know that. Thank you."

"We'd better get going. The more distance we put between us and the action, the better off we'll be. We'll travel until we're out of light. I didn't get you all out just to have you fall off a mountain in the dark."

"Yes, sir."

By the time darkness made its appearance we were almost to the top. We found a shelf large enough to camp on and bedded down for night. I took care of the horses, then went over to where Sara and Kate were tending to Billie.

They had her shirt up around her neck and she wasn't shy about it. There were some bruises on her breasts and on her side.

"Anything broken?" I asked.

Kate was feeling around and answered, "I don't think so. I think she's just bruised up some."

"I'll be all right," Billie assured us.

"Okay, let's get some rest. I want to get down off this mountain by midday."

It was cold and brought back memories of another night Sara and I had spent on the mountain together. She came over to lie down next to me.

"Just for warmth," she told me. "Kate's staying with Billie."

"Okay," I told her, wrapping my arms around her and covering us both with my blanket, "just for warmth."

"What are you going to do when we get down off this hill?" she asked.

"I'm going back to Baxterville," I told her.

"For your wagon?"

"For Dade Whitman, too. I've got a score to settle with him."

"You could get yourself killed," she told me.

"That's a possibility, but I've got to go back to get my wagon, and I'm not going to be able to leave that town without paying him a visit. I owe it to him."

"Because he sent all those men after us?"

"Yeah," I told her, "and for a lot of other things, things in the past."

"What about us?"

"Sara, that's something you and Kate and Billie are going to have to discuss. Where you're going to go, what you're going to do. The only suggestion I have right now is that whatever you decide, you stay together, at least for a while."

I felt her nod her head against my chest.

"That sounds like a good idea," she agreed.

"There is one place I can drop you off at," I told her.

"Where's that?"

"It's actually on my way to Baxterville."

"Is it in Mexico?"

"Yes."

"Well, where? What kind of place is it?"

"It's called St. Augustine."

"Is it a town?"

I shook my head.

"A mission, then?"

I shook my head again.

"Don't tell me—" she began, then broke off with a short laugh.

"Yeah," I told her. "It's a convent."

36

The nuns at St. Augustine welcomed Mrs. Macklin and her two young daughters. They assured me that they would treat the injuries the younger girl received when she fell off her horse.

They took Billie to a room upstairs, while I said goodbye to Kate and Sara.

"I don't suppose we'll ever meet again," Kate told me. She kissed me lightly on the mouth. "Thanks, Clint, and good luck." She went upstairs to make sure Billie was cared for. Sara walked me outside. She wanted to say goodbye to Duke.

"So long, big boy," she told him, patting his nose affectionately. She gave him some sugar, probably the last he'd get for a while.

Then she turned to me.

"I've got no sugar for you," she told me.

I gathered her up and kissed her the way you're supposed to kiss a woman when you're saying goodbye.

"Clint, I—" she started, her eyes filling with tears.

"Goodbye, Sara. Let's just say goodbye," I suggested.

"And good luck."

I nodded and got up on Duke.

I had taken one of the other horses as a pack-horse, and the good sisters had been kind enough to give me some food and coffee. Traveling alone was a lot easier than traveling with three women. I was even able to ride at night and made it from Mexico to Missouri in half the time it had taken us to get from Missouri to Mexico.

I arranged it so I'd arrive in Baxterville after dark. By now Whitman would have the town in the palm of his hand, and he'd have enough deputies to keep it there.

I eased Duke on up to the rear of the livery where my rig was supposed to be. I hoped it was still there and that Whitman hadn't seen fit to get rid of it in anticipation of my death. If it was there, he'd probably have a man sitting on it every night, in the event that I would return, because he knew that if I came back, I'd be coming for him.

I went to Lizzie's house and tapped on her window. She looked out and broke into a big smile when she saw me. I met her at the back door and she threw her arms around me and smothered me with a kiss that took my breath away.

"You're back!" she breathed.

"Let's keep it quiet, though," I warned her. "Nobody is supposed to know."

"Okay. You wanna come in? Pa's away."

"I can't. Listen, Lizzie, I need your help."

"Sure," she said, rubbing herself against me. "I'll help you all I can."

"Has Whitman taken over the town yet?"

"He sure has, him and his deputies. In some ways, he's even worse than Macklin was."

"That much I knew. Look, I have to get into the livery."

"He's got a man in there," she told me. "Puts one in there every night."

"That's what I figured. Let me have the key to the lock on the back door, and then go back to bed. Don't tell anyone you saw me."

"Okay, wait a minute." She went inside and came back out with the key. "Will you come back and see me?" she asked.

"If I can. Now get back inside."

She kissed me and ran back in.

I went back to the livery and fitted the key into the lock as quietly as I could. I took the lock and the chain off the door and set it on the ground.

I took out my gun and eased the door open enough for me to slip through. The gun was a precaution. I didn't want to use it because that would announce my presence to Whitman. This was one of the times I wished I carried a knife.

I could see the silhouette of my wagon. My guess was that they had been waiting for me for so long that they had probably taken to sleeping in the back of the wagon. I stayed still a few moments and eventually I could make out the deep, even breathing of a man asleep. He died the easiest way there is to die. He went to sleep, and he never woke up.

My next move was Whitman. In all the years I'd known him, he'd always used the sheriff's office for his own personal use, so I knew I'd find him there.

The streets of the town were dark and deserted. Knowing Whitman, he had probably imposed a curfew. All I had to look out for was one of his "deputies."

I made it to his office without running into anyone. Gun in hand, I turned the doorknob and stepped in. I had the gun trained on his desk, but he wasn't behind it. A quick look left and right told me that the room was totally empty. That left the back, where the cells were. The door was wide open, and I couldn't hear anyone, prisoner or otherwise. Chances were pretty good at this point that he was back there sleeping in one of the cells.

I kept my gun ready as I crossed the room to the open metal door. I stayed quiet, as I had in the livery, searching for the sounds of a man asleep. I couldn't hear any, but I stayed careful and stepped into the room quietly.

There were four cells, and I found him in the last one. He was lying on one of the cots, face up. His eyes were open, but they stared sightlessly at the ceiling. I touched his face and found the flesh still fairly warm. There was a rope around his neck, which was barely visible because the flesh had swelled up around it.

He'd been strangled by someone very strong.

I holstered my gun and considered my situation. I may have come back to Baxterville to kill Dade Whitman, but that was neither here nor there right now. He was already dead. As far as who had killed him, there was only one other man I knew of who had a good enough reason to kill him. No doubt Whitman had plenty of enemies in his past, but recently he'd gotten on the wrong side of two men.

I was one man. Con Macklin was the other. That meant that Con Macklin was still alive.

I didn't know how he had managed it, but he had to have escaped being captured or killed by the Federales.

He must have figured things the same way that I did and come up with Dade Whitman as the man who tipped off the Mexicans. It couldn't have been me, because there was no way I could have gotten a message out of that valley.

Why'd Whitman betray Macklin? One reason was fairly easy to figure: Dade Whitman was just plain mean. Another reason was probably self-preservation, to keep Macklin from ever coming back and reclaiming his town. Then there was the fact that Whitman had been unable to come up with Macklin's money. That must have frustrated him. He probably figured he could get us all killed at the same time by letting the Mexican government do his dirty work for him.

Now it had all backfired on him.

I had something else to worry about now.

Where was Macklin? Was I his next victim? Whitman's body was still warm, which meant Macklin had been there fairly recently. Was he still in town, waiting for me to show up? Or was he gone, satisfied with having killed Whitman?

I figured him to be gone. The town was still full of Dade Whitman's men. Macklin had gotten lucky. He'd been able to get in, kill Whitman and then get out again. He wasn't the kind of man to push his luck. He'd be satisfied with what he got this time and settle up with me another time.

Still, I left Whitman's office very carefully, keeping to the shadows. I made my way back to the livery and hitched my team to my wagon. I tied Duke to the back of the wagon and then walked the rig out of town. Once I was reasonably clear I jumped up into the wagon and got going.

I was sorry I hadn't gotten a chance to see Lizzie again, but I couldn't take the chance. I was sure she'd understand. In fact, she'd probably understand for the wrong reason, figuring I was the one who killed Whitman and that I'd had to light out.

When Whitman's men found him they'd probably turn the town upside down looking for someone to blame, but that wouldn't last long. The paymaster was dead, and with no one to pay them they'd probably scatter and leave town. The people of Baxterville would get their town back once again. I only hoped that this time they'd be more careful with it.

Whitman was dead and I was satisfied. As far as I was concerned I had no further business with Con Macklin. He could go his way and I'd go mine.

It wasn't that big a country, really. We'd probably run into each other again . . . someday.

I didn't realize how soon it would be.

37

San Francisco was a city I tried to see at least once a year. I made it four months after I left Baxterville. I put my rig up with a friend and rode Duke into town. I had made out pretty well, financially, from the Macklin thing. I'd made four hundred for guiding the ladies, plus what I'd made from poker while I was in Macklin's Valley.

I stayed in one of the better hotels, ate at the best restaurants, and went to see the better shows. I like to get away from the West once in a while, and the only way to get away from the West without going back East is to go to San Francisco.

I made the acquaintance of several ladies of breeding, did some gambling, and just generally relaxed.

One night I got involved in an expensive backroom poker game, where the conversation eventually turned to the new "house of entertainment" in San Francisco.

"Gentlemen, you wouldn't believe the ladies that abide there," one dandy was saying. He could afford to talk, since he was one of the two winners in the game.

I was the other.

"When did you say this place opened up?" I asked, regarding with fondness the two kings that I had in the hole. There was another bearded gentleman sitting on the table with two little deuces, which gave me a lovely full house. I figured the dandy with the money, who was doing the talking, might have a full house also, but his was destined to be lower than mine, because two of the other players had folded with aces.

"Three, perhaps four months ago," he told me. "Queens bet a hundred," he said, pushing a hundred-dollars worth of chips toward the center of the table. He had queens on board, and I figured him for a third in the hole. As in the case of the aces, his fourth queen had been folded long ago with someone else's hand.

"I'll see your hundred, and raise you two," I told him, shoveling the chips forward.

The only other player left in the hand promptly folded, and the dandy regarded his cards for a moment, then said, "I believe I will bump you just once, sir, to see how serious you are."

He raised me two hundred.

I showed him how serious I was by raising him five hundred dollars.

"Well, sir, I guess you were very serious. I also believe that I will let you have the pot and be off," he told me, throwing his in. "I think that I shall call it a night here and be off in search of other entertainment."

"You wouldn't be going to that establishment you were just talking about, would you?" I asked, pulling in my chips.

"I believe I will stop there on my way to the hotel, yes. Would you care to join me?"

"I believe I will, thank you."

In spite of having lost that final hand, the dandy still came out a winner, as I saw when we both cashed in our chips. Similarly encumbered by newly-acquired wealth, we inspected the streets outside very carefully before proceeding down them.

"Bill, you son of a gun," I said when we were far enough away.

"Hello, Clint."

"You sure can talk like an Easterner when you want to, can't you, you old weasel," I remarked.

"When I'm dressed like a genteel gambler, that's how people 'spect me to act. I don't aim to disappoint them. Hell, when I saw you walk into that game I just 'bout shouted. I knew we could take those dandys for all they was worth, and by God, we did it."

We were passing a saloon and I said, "Let's go in here and have a drink."

It wasn't one of the higher-class saloons in San Francisco, but then Bill and I did most of our drinking out of dirty glasses.

"What happened to you after Anadarko?" I asked him.

"Well, I traveled a bit with that young Mr. Earp, but after a spell he started getting me depressed. You know moonin' about his dead wife and all. We parted company after a couple of weeks. I traveled some, got into a scrape or two, then decided it was time for some genteel living, so I came out here. What about you?"

I gave him the whole story, from beginning to end. He sat back and hooked his thumbs in his fancy vest and observed, "Seems to me Whitman did you a good turn without wanting to. If those Federales hadn't hit when they did, you'd've been dead."

I raised my glass and said, "Here's to Dade Whitman, then."

Bill raised his glass and said, "May he burn."

"Now, what about this new place you were telling me about?" I asked, "or was that part of the act?"

"No act, by golly. In fact, come to think of it, you might be very interested in this place at that." He slapped his knee and said, "Damn, but I knew that lady looked familiar."

"What lady?"

"The one what runs this cathouse."

"Familiar from where?" I asked, pouring myself another drink and lifting the glass to my lips.

"Anadarko. She's the same redhead who was with you that day," he told me.

I spilled my drink on the table and stared at him. "Kate?"

"If that's her name. Here she calls herself Katherine, and she runs the finest whorehouse on the coast."

38

Bill gave me directions, but begged off as far as coming with me. He had a lady lined-up somewhere else. He gave me the name of his hotel and I told him I'd try to see him again before one of us left town.

I took a carriage to Kate's place, and was very impressed when he delivered me to the doorstep.

"Finest women in San Francisco," the driver told me with a leer.

"I've heard," I told him.

The house was huge, all lit up with lights and activity. There was a policeman stationed out front for the purpose of protection. He was obviously protecting Kate's best interests and being paid very handsomely for it, too.

I tipped my hat to him and ascended the front steps.

Where had Kate managed to come up with the money to open a place like this, I had no idea.

I was met at the door by a young hostess wearing a very expensive, brightly-colored gown with a bodice cut low enough to offer a decent view of her high breasts.

"Is this your first time with us, sir?" she asked.

"It is."

"My name is Lindsay," she told me. "Would you be kind enough to tell me who referred you?"

I was about to give her Bill's name when I thought better of it.

"The sisters of St. Augustine," I told her.

The smile on her face froze for a moment and she looked closer at me and asked, "I beg your pardon?"

"The sisters of—never mind. Would you be kind enough to tell Miss Katherine that I'd like to see her?" I asked.

"Miss Katherine doesn't usually see the, uh, customers, sir. We can offer you a wide variety of—"

"I'd rather see Kate."

"Kate?" she said, her smile slipping again.

"I'm an old friend of hers," I explained.

"Who shall I tell her—"

"Tell her it's the Gunsmith."

She was undecided between calling the policeman outside, or delivering my message to Kate, so I took out twenty dollars and tucked it in the warm, fragrant valley between her white breasts. Her attitude changed abruptly.

"I'll give her the message, sir. Please sit and wait?"

I decided to remain standing and watched her ascend the staircase to the second floor. I was approached by two or three very lovely young ladies, and under normal circumstances would certainly have succumbed to one of them.

"Clint!" I heard a voice call from the head of the stairs. I looked up and it was Kate. Her red hair was piled atop her head, as it had been when we first met. The sequined gown she wore clung to the top portion of her body and flaired out over those lovely hips and thighs that I remembered so well. She ran down the steps and I caught her in my arms. She kissed me deeply and then stepped back.

"You look marvelous. How did you find me?"

"I wasn't looking," I admitted. "I just happen to be in

town and heard about your place. I knew it was you from the description."

"Word has gotten around quickly. We're a smashing success."

"So I've heard. How've you been?"

"I'm grand. Oh, let's go upstairs and talk. Lindsay," she said to the hostess, "a bottle of champagne to my room please."

"Yes, ma'am," the girl said.

"Come with me," she told me, grabbing my hand and leading me up the stairs. Her room was extravagantly furnished with expensive pieces of furniture, some of which she told me were genuine antiques. The champagne was brought by a black man in a dark suit who poured two glasses and left.

"To old adventures," she told me, raising her glass. We clinked glasses and drank.

"What happened after St. Augustine?" I asked her.

"We stayed awhile, discussing what we should do, where we should go. I wanted to come to San Francisco, Sara said she wanted to travel to Europe. Billie—well, Billie stayed with the sisters."

I stared at her disbelievingly.

"Billie stayed at the convent?" I asked.

She nodded, smiling.

"She said she'd never felt so much at peace, so she decided to stay."

"I'm glad for her," I said after a moment. "Maybe she's finally happy. And Sara?"

She leaned forward, giving me a tantalizing view of her large breasts and said, "We'll talk about Sara later."

We were seated on her antique sofa and I took her in my arms and kissed her.

"Kate, where did you ever get the money—" I started to ask, and then it hit me. She saw that I understood and her eyes went down demurely.

"Oh, Kate," I said, scolding her, "you held out on me."

"I'm sorry—"

"That other sack you were carrying. Those 'personal things' that you didn't want to leave behind. You took Macklin's money!"

"Yes, I did."

"Do you realize that he would never have stopped looking for us when he realized that you had his money?" I asked her.

"I know, but I couldn't just leave it there." She poured some more champagne and said, "Besides, with Con dead—"

"Oh," I said, realizing that she didn't know what I knew.

"What does that mean?" she asked.

So I told her about Dade Whitman, and how I was sure that Macklin wasn't dead. She looked like she was going to go into shock.

"That means he may still—"

"Easy, Kate. Chances are good you'll never see him again. How could he find you?"

"You did, and you weren't even looking," she reminded me.

She had a point there.

"Look, Kate, let's not let bad thoughts spoil our reunion," I told her.

"Our reunion," she repeated, then looked at me and said, "Oh, reunion!" She put her glass down and said, "Look, Clint, I'm going to be busy for a while yet. I'll have Lindsay put you in one of the other rooms. I'll send you my best girl, and then when I'm finished you can come back here and we'll have our reunion properly."

"Kate—" I began, wondering what the rush was all of a sudden.

"Wait here," she told me. She went out of the room,

leaving me a little bewildered, and in a few moments Lindsay came in and said, "Will you come this way, please?"

I shrugged and followed her to another room. I might as well enjoy myself, I thought, since it was probably all on the house.

The room she took me to was not as extravagantly furnished as Kate's, but it was still mighty impressive.

"Make yourself comfortable, Mr. Adams. Sally will be with you in a moment."

"Sally?"

"Yes, sir. Please, Kate wants you to be comfortable."

"Thank you."

She disappeared and I was left alone. I took off my jacket and my gunbelt, then sat on the bed to remove my boots. While I was working on that the door opened and someone stepped in.

"Let me help with those," a familiar female voice said.

I looked up and saw Sara standing by the door, wearing a filmy nightgown that hid none of her magnificent curves.

"Hello, Clint," she said. I stood up and she rushed into my arms. I kissed her, deep and long, the way you should kiss a woman when you say hello.

She hugged me tightly and whispered, "I've missed you."

"I missed you, too," I admitted.

I was about to say more, but she silenced me with her fingers and said, "No more talk for a while."

She stepped back and allowed the nightgown to fall to the floor. If anything she seemed to have improved during the past four months. Her breasts were marvelous, firm white globes, tipped with pink. Her waist was impossibly trim for a big woman, and her hips and thighs were perfect. She approached me and bore me down to the bed. I began kissing her breasts, sucking on the nipples, and she told me, "Hurry, darling, please hurry. We'll go slow later."

I undressed and we made frenzied, passionate love, like two people who haven't seen each other in four months and have missed one another.

Afterward as we lay together she told me, "Billie's happy, Kate's happy, now I'm happy."

"What happened to Europe?"

She shrugged.

"Maybe later, when I have someone to go with," she told me.

"Sara, did you know that Kate had Macklin's money when we left?" I asked her.

She shook her head. "I didn't know until after you left us at the convent, I swear, Clint."

I believed her.

As the night went on I chose my moment and then told her about Con Macklin being alive.

"How can you be sure?" she asked.

"Who else had reason to kill Whitman?" I asked her. "I felt it, Sara, and I still feel it. He's alive."

"And he's out there somewhere," she said, "Looking for us."

"I told Kate and I'll tell you. He'll probably never find you. It's a big country."

"You found us, and—"

"—I wasn't even looking. I know, that's what Kate said."

"Let's forget Con Macklin, Clint," she said, rolling atop me. "Let's forget everyone but us."

I kissed her and ran my hands down her back to her buttocks. She moved her hips and I had just glided into the sweet, warm depths of her when someone knocked on the door.

"They'll go away," she whispered to me.

The knock came again.

"Go away," Sara called out.

"Sally, please. It's Lindsay. I have to see Mr. Adams."

Sara raised her eyebrows at me and said, "Another conquest?"

"I never touched her. I swear."

She rolled off of me, got up and put on a robe. It was obvious we were in her room.

She opened the door and let Lindsay in.

"This better be good," she told her, but her tone was warm, not cold.

"It's Katherine," she told us. "Mr. Adams, something's wrong." She was very frightened.

"Calm down, Lindsay. Tell me what happened."

"A man came in and asked for her, a big man, mean-looking. When she saw him she got scared. He took her to her room and they locked the door." She looked at Sara, as if apologizing, and said, "I listened at the door. They were shouting at each other, then I heard her cry out."

Sara looked at me and said, "It's him, Clint. I know it's him."

"Easy, Sara," I said, getting up, ignoring the fact that I was naked. I started to get dressed and asked Lindsay, "How long ago was this?"

"About fifteen minutes. I'm so scared."

"Stay here with Sar—Sally, Lindsay." To Sara I said, "Don't come out of this room. Lock the door until you hear my voice."

I ignored my boots and buckled on my gun.

"Lock it," I said again, and left the room. I waited until I heard the lock click, then made my way down to Kate's room.

I listened at the door and I could hear voices, I couldn't make out what they were saying, but they were angry voices. And then I heard the sound of a blow being struck.

I backed up and kicked the door in.

They both froze the way they were. Macklin, looking mean, dirty and unshaven, standing over Kate, who was on the floor, holding her cheek.

"Well," Macklin said slowly, "It looks like I hit the jackpot. All the traitors in one little basket."

His gun was in his holster, as was mine. That seemed fair.

"You're wrong, Con," I told him. "In order to be a traitor, you first have to be loyal. We were never loyal to you."

"Well, that makes you even worse. Pretendin' to be loyal when all the time you wanted my women and my money."

"He didn't take the money, Con," Kate told him quickly. "I did. Clint didn't even know I had it."

"Listen to her, tryin' to save your life. Hidin' behind women now, Adams?" he asked nastily.

"I'm not hiding, Con," I said, raising my left hand, but keeping my right by my gun. "I'm standing right here. Your gun is in your holster, and so is mine. Make your move."

I was going to have to kill him. If I didn't, he could always come back for them.

"You think you can take me, Adams? You're crazy."

I didn't answer. I was watching his eyes.

"I don't even want this whore," he said, indicating Kate. "I want my money . . . and Sara."

"I'd give you the money if I had it, Con, but I'd never give you Sara. You'll have to kill me to get her."

"Then I will."

He turned his head to look at Kate, but that was to throw me off. As his head turned, his hand went for his gun.

Up until this day I had only seen one man go for his gun whose hand I couldn't follow every inch of the way. That's how I know I've got a man beat. When I can see his hand moving, like it was moving in slow motion, I know I've got all the time in the world. The only man whose hand I could never follow was Bill, and I thanked God I'd never have to draw against him.

Macklin was fast, there was no doubt about that, but as soon as his hand started to move I knew I had him. I had time to look at Kate, look at him, see the sweat on his brow and the sneer on his lips before I finally went for my gun, and I still cleared leather way before he did.

The bullet caught him in the chest and lifted him off the ground. The sneer left his lips and was replaced by a round "O" of surprise. The pain crept into his eyes for a moment, but then he died before he hit the floor, and when he did his face was blank.

Con Macklin was finally dead. For real.

39

The policeman outside saw to it that Macklin's body was carted away with a minimum of fanfare. That was one of the things he was paid to do, Kate told me.

After Macklin was taken away Kate, Sara and I sat on that antique couch in Kate's room.

"Now it's over," I told them.

"Finally."

"Will you stay?" Sara asked, knowing the answer even as she asked.

"I don't know, Sara."

"How about that trip to Europe?" she asked.

"It sounds nice," I told her. "Why don't we sleep on it."

"All of us," Kate said. "It's time to close so we can all get to sleep."

She chased us out of her room and kissed us both. As I left she grabbed my arm and said, "I'm always thanking you, Clint."

"Let's hope this is the last time it's necessary," I told her.

I went back to Sara's room and we made love again, reveling in the fact that we were both alive. When she had finally fallen asleep I sat up in bed and looked at her. She had become, little by little and aided by the four months we hadn't seen each other, the most beautiful woman I had ever been with. If I had to tie myself to someone I could do worse, I told myself.

She, however, could do better, so it was time for me to leave San Francisco.

My reasons for leaving were not totally unselfish, however. As I rode Duke out of San Francisco and headed for who-knew-where, I realized that, as beautiful as Sara was, I could never tie myself to any one person, or any one place. That might even be the reason I had given up my star. Wearing it tied me to one town, or one county. After all those years as a lawman, I had caught the wanderlust.

That's a mighty hard thing to get rid of.